Faith Orion's Field

a novel by
Michelle Cushing

MULBERRY BARK

A MULBERRY BARK BOOK

Published by
Mulberry Bark Publishing

PUBLISHER'S NOTE
This book is a work of fiction. Names, characters, places, and incidents either are products of the author's imagination or are used fictitiously. Any resemblance to actual events or locales or persons, living or dead, is entirely coincidental.

For information contact Mulberry Bark Publishing.
http://www.mulberrybark.com

ISBN: 978-0-9796935-3-3

Printed in the United States of America

First Edition

MULBERRY❦BARK

For my family:
both the crazy and the sane, those walking on land, the
ones living among the stars, and those I have yet to meet ...

Disclaimer:
Please use caution before picking or consuming
any unfamiliar berry as certain ones are poisonous.

Chapter 1

We have a saying in my family – embrace the crazy. Grandma Dunley embraced it at every opportunity. You see, it's like this, everyone in my family needs a straight jacket. The most industrial one they can make. Something that would have confounded even Houdini. Except me. Not good ol' stable Faith. I fought the crazy both tooth and nail, which is an expression Granny D always said, too. You have to fight everything "tooth and nail." Any hardship, take it on tooth and nail. It doesn't even make sense, but it is an accurate description of Granny D. Tough as tooth and nails.

I half-expected her to be waiting for me at the train station, but she couldn't do that. She was in jail. The police station is a little ways outside of town and services three small, rural areas. The only way to get to Mulberry Field, Arkansas is via the train. You can fly into Little Rock and drive the rest of the way, but for as long as I can remember this is how it's done. Go northeast, past Keo, past Scott and you'll find it. Small farming community dotted sparsely with big brick homes of the farmers doing well and trailers for the ones who are not. There are vast endless fields of cotton, the main commodity of the people in town for generations. Busted barns, dilapidated rusted silos, scraggly dogs, and kids on bicycles aren't exactly scenic, but you'll see it everywhere you look. There's a Safeway, a Subway, a Little Caesars Pizza, and a video rental place called BlockMaster, a terrible rip-off of the popular chain, but I'm sure they would find Mulberry Field a scooch too small to actually open a store. The only things in the town center are a post office and a community center. One strip mall is nearby that houses a beauty salon, flower shop, and both a discount shoe store and dress shop. The schools are lined up like a strip mall too. All three are right next to one another. Graduating from elementary school, you move over to the next building. If you need groceries and don't want the hassle of Safeway, then there is always Maude's, the local mom-and-pop shop owned by a woman who has to be at least one hundred years old with boobs that hang low like two potatoes in a pair of pantyhose. The rest of the town is littered with a couple of gas stations, which are still known as "fillin' stations" to many of the elderly locals. One service station is used by everyone, Edward Field's Auto Repair. He can fix anything. He's probably close to one hundred years old, too. You get the feeling he could probably fix a Model T. Then, of course, there is the train station, a one platform strip of tracks on your way to someplace else. It's managed by a guy named Bob. He has a toothless smile, but wears an immaculately pressed suit that looks like something Buster Keaton would have worn in the 1920s. Impressed with it, Granny D always called the outfit "smart."

Some people might think what my Granny D did wasn't too smart. She was hauled in for flying her pajama bottoms up an abandoned flag pole on Mulberry Pointe, the highest hillside in town. Some say it's an Indian burial mound, but it's really just a big bump in the ground, the remnants of a very old construction site. There's a forgotten flag pole atop it, and that's where Granny D flies her PJs every year to signal the sale of her mulberry jam, but it wasn't jam and jelly season this time around. My mother had succumbed to lupus.

I was at the office when I got the news. My secretary Brad thinks every phone call must be taken immediately. Taking a message is a mortal sin. If they take the time to call, he believes I should take the time to answer. I'm usually too busy to take calls. That's why I have Brad. He's normally pained when I ask him to take a message, but he ran into my office as if the place were on fire. My grandmother had been arrested. "Arrested!" he had yelled like I should have passed out at the thought. I took the call, calmly. That's how I found out Mama had died. Can you imagine being so out of touch with your family that you didn't realize your own mother was dying?

The air that day had smelled heavily of gasoline fumes. I couldn't get the scent out of my nose. It was like every bus in Boston puffed out an unimaginable amount of billowy black smog. It choked the ozone. It choked me. I couldn't walk down the street fast enough. I had to go home.

Mulberries have a very distinct scent. Not like a grape or a blueberry. Sweet and tart all at once, it wafts up your nose slowly like the smell of ham cooking on Christmas morning, slowly permeating the house, knowing damned well it's all you can think about. You have to taste it. I've grown up with that scent, mulberries stewing for jam. They grow wild in Mulberry Field, hence the name. Step off the train and there it is, right up your nose. Don't fight it; it stays in your clothes, on your skin. I swear it's even colored my black hair. I've been told I have a uniquely fruity smell, which I've fought for many years by musking and husking it up with perfume.

When I stepped onto the train platform in Mulberry Field, I took in a deep breath. I didn't smell bus butt smoke, or expensive cologne, or exotic cooking. Just mulberries. The way it always has been.

I wished someone had been waiting for me at the station. I had to ask Ol' man Wilson to drive me. If you are ancient enough to have shared your childhood with my grandparents, then you are instantly referred to as "Ol' man such and such," except for the elderly women. They have names. And Bob from the train station. He's just Bob. Not sure why that is. Ol' man Wilson is the only cabbie in town which means he spends most of his time socializing and drinking cherry limeades at the Sonic a few miles outside of town. The train arrives and leaves once a day, and Ol' man Wilson waits on anyone who needs a ride. He's shriveled like a worm dying on a hot sidewalk, but unlike the big city drivers, he's friendly, his cab is clean, and he doesn't smell of chutney. He smells like beer. I don't know why that is either, and I tried not think of it as I got into the cab, a former race car that once belonged to Arkansas driver Jim Harper with the number three fading on the doors.

He offered me his condolences. Everyone knows everyone here. It's like everyone lives up everyone else's butt. One sneeze and via a chain of phone calls the entire town will rhapsodize "bless you" like a chorus. He had been up to see Granny D just the other day and had given her a bushel of apples from his orchard. His wife was Granny D's best friend Bertha, who was Poppy D's sister. God rest their souls, Granny D always laments when referring to anyone deceased, but I don't recall her drawing the PJs up the flagpole for either of them. I don't recall Granny doing that for anyone.

"Saw your show the other day," he said to me after I got situated in the car. Everyone here has seen my show. I'm a local celebrity. I'm a national celebrity. My cooking show runs every Tuesday on FWC, The FoodWorks Channel. I cook hoity-toity food that no one in Mulberry Field would bother to attempt.

"Not sure 'bout that 'rugula though. Never tried that," he said with a genuine smile.

"Arugula, yes. You should. You'd like it. A little spicy."

"I can't eat spicy much anymore. Or corn. Shame."

I've found that old people have a problem with corn. It never seems to digest well. Does it for anyone? So I told him so. He laughed. I was laughing and my mother had just died.

The last time I saw Mama in Mulberry Field was the day I went off to college twenty years ago. Dark hair tucked neatly under a wide-brimmed hat, she sat on a bench at the station with my sister Gracie Ann, who flipped me off playfully behind Mama's back. Granny D and Poppy D had held hands, joyous and buoyant and oblivious to the importance of that moment. Mama had this bizarre mixture of sadness and happiness (for me) on her face. She knew the importance of the moment. Faith Orion would not return. Bound for Harvard to study English literature, then off to Le Cordon Bleu in Paris, I was an up-and-coming chef with my future in my hands like a pile of delicate fillo dough that I could shape into whatever I desired.

Mama never left Mulberry Field. She's part of the landscape now, or part of the night sky. When I was a child, Granny D used to tell me that the dead go up to heaven, up to the stars. As I rode with Ol' man Wilson, the stars hid behind the daylight sky, merging on the horizon with the endless fields.

Chapter 2

When I got home I could smell it. Not mulberries. Ham.
Granny D was already out of the lock-up. She came out on the porch
carrying a screwdriver.

"Damned things busted again," she said. Pissed. This woman
has hot sorghum running through her veins – heavy, sticky, and not as
sweet as you think. Her arms were waving, but her smile was friendly.
"Barney Wilson, you pickin' up my grandbaby in that fuckin' jalopy?
You should've driven Bertha's car. You knew Faith was comin' in
today."

"Marly, I told ya. Bertha's car don't run no more," he said,
helping me with my bags. Being my grandmother's brother-in-law
gave him the right to call her Marly. Most people call her Granny D.
For some reason, I imagine they may have even called her that when
she was a kid, but she started out Marlene Averton Prescott. Very
snooty sounding, but the reality was not. She grew up a dirt poor only
child who kicked her way to survival. She fought for Uncle Sam, for

peace, for women, and for civil liberties. Injustice infuriated her. Telling someone they couldn't do something, or didn't have the right to do something, put her over the roof. She had worked at the county school board, once started a coalition for Native Americans in town because she believed they were being treated unjustly, and staged a sit-in when her favorite hair salon raised the price of a haircut by five dollars. None of this made her famous though. She was famous for her cooking way before I was born. My food ended up on television. Her meals were the stuff of legends.

"Get in here and help me with this," she told Ol' man Wilson. Granny D rarely "said" anything. She "told" you to do something and you did it. "I can't reach up under there. You have tiny little hands. You do it," she added.

"I do not have tiny hands," he replied.

He did actually.

Granny D held out her arms as I came up the steps. "My baby, come home," she said and hugged me heartily before looking me over. "Look at you, you're skin and bones." This is another one of her expressions, "skin and bones," which I am far from. I'm on the pudgy side like my dad. It's Granny D that looks like skin and bones. She has the bone structure of a wire hanger. She looks frail but that is a deception.

"It's the refrigerator," she said to Ol' man Wilson as he came up behind me. "I got the thing pulled out from the wall, but I can't reach where I need to. Same things as always with that piece of work."

"You need to buy new," he told her, hauling my bags inside after us.

"You need a new fridge, Granny?" I asked. "I can get you one. Why didn't you tell me?"

"This one's fine."

It was not fine. With a rusty stain on the front, the ugly blue thing was old and ready to be retired. It was still covered with the same magnets from my childhood – black-n-white milk cow, apple, and ear of corn with the green leaf top broken off. In my opinion this wasn't a refrigerator. It was never a refrigerator. It was an "icebox," some bizarre remnant from the past that you'd say, "Well, would you look at that," if you spotted it in a flea market.

I think people might say the same thing if they saw where I grew up. When you pull into the same splat of land that my grandparents lived on since marriage, you always park your car in the back. Closer to the kitchen. The back porch is open, airy, and wraps all around the house. The front porch, however, is screened in. It is only used when you want to sip tea outside without mosquitoes biting you. The house is not big or small, just average, but it is bright yellow. The land outside is green and vast. When I arrived I noticed the garden was flourishing, but my old tire swing was rotting, rooted in time. No dust stirred on the long driveway in the back. Technically, it is a road. The 911 emergency people thought it needed a name in case there was ever a crisis and they couldn't find us. So, I grew up on Astral Lane, my sister's choice. Really, though, it is just a driveway, always will be, and it leads to my childhood home behind my grandparent's house. I cannot distinguish between these two residences. It is all one property with two homes, thirteen acres of trees (pine, oak, and mulberry), and one workable field.

I never talked about where I came from too much. As a popular television chef with scores of cookbooks to my credit, I didn't think the average viewer would appreciate my time in the "boons," boondocks, which is how I had often referred to it. My ex-husband Stephan understood, but he didn't quite grasp my upbringing. It was foreign to him. I had met Stephan in France; his family was refined. I always saw myself as refined, but my "embrace the crazy" family was not dignified. They went into the woods barefoot to pick berries. Stephan's family owned a vineyard. I wanted my family to serve brie and drink wine, but we ate homemade biscuits and drank sweet tea. Wee Ste-fan, as his French-English mother nicknamed him for his tiny stature, was always the picture of European elegance with his perfectly coiffed hair, dainty hands, and a pair of black loafers so polished I could see my reflection in them. When Granny D had met him at our wedding, she scoffed. "He's not a full-sized man," she had said. "Too short. He needs to be put back in the oven to puff up like a wad of dough."

Our families never really got to know one another too well though. I kept my upbringing from most of my French friends, but I think Wee Ste-fan would have gotten along with my father. Dad died when I was about four years old. Massive coronary. Too much ham. Mama said Dad never saw it coming. He never saw anything coming. Neither did Wee Ste-fan. Like my father, Stephan lived in some happyland without problems, their heads filled with bubblegum and candy canes like kids in *'Twas the Night Before Christmas*. They were both writers. Wee Ste-fan wrote travel guides based on food, where to find the best eateries, the best prices, the fanciest or most exquisite of tastes. Dad wrote books on appliance repair. You know those do-it-yourself books you see in the library about how to fix a stove or how to redo your bathroom? He wrote those. He could have fixed the icebox without problem.

"Marly," Ol' man Wilson said, "you're going to have to buy new."

"Oh, hell. I am not. I'll get Eddie over here." She looked around, pondering the situation, not wanting to admit the refrigerator had won this battle. "Let's move everything to the freezer."

Ol' man Wilson and I helped Granny D move everything to the storage room just to the back of the kitchen which used to be my Uncle John's bedroom. Granny stored everything back there. Shelves are always lined with jams and any vegetable you can pickle. Boxes are filled with jars to be steamed and sanitized. Pectin stacked neatly on a table. Several bags of fresh purple hull peas were on the floor. Not everything is kitchen-related back here though. There is a broken chair and a painting hanging upside down of Buster, our one-eyed, three-legged cat from childhood. My sister Gracie Ann painted it at age ten. Despite his disabilities, that cat is the ancestor of about a third of the kitten population in Mulberry Field.

We opened the freezer and I knew what would be in there. Ice cream sandwiches. There were always ice cream sandwiches. I took one out and opened it. Famous chefs be damned, my favorite dessert is still an ice cream sandwich.

"Isn't she skin and bones?" Granny D said to Wilson.

"Wastin' away," he replied.

I smiled. "Then I'll have two," I said, plucking another out of the freezer.

It took about an hour to get everything from the refrigerator into the freezer. Granny D is a perfectionist when it comes to kitchen goods. I know that's where I get it. Everything has to be "just so."

"Milk's going to be a solid block," Granny D said to me after we were done and Ol' man Wilson had gone home. "I hope you don't want cereal in the morning."

We had spent all that time already and not one mention of Mama yet. I'm not sure if it was me or her avoiding the subject. I felt a warm, wet nose sniffing around my ankles and saw Jake, Granny D's black pug, at my heels. He snorted when I reached down to pet him. He must have realized I'm a cat person.

"Jakey, let's help Faith put her things in her old bedroom." She picked up my bags and nodded with her head for us to get a move on. Whenever my sister or I had a fight with our mom, or just wanted to sleep over, then we used my mother's old room. I used it more than Gracie Ann, so it really became "my" bedroom. It looks exactly the same to this very day. A poster of *The Breakfast Club*, green-and-gold pom-poms, and CDs by INXS.

"Wash your hands. We have ham," Granny D said and left me alone with my teenage remnants. "I need you to run up to Eddie's. He already has a part for the tractor for me, and I want him to look at the fridge. Can't go without a fridge."

Jake followed her back through the house. I sat down on the bed. I needed another ice cream sandwich really bad. I didn't want ham. I didn't want food like that. It was too heavy. Sweet, light, frozen was all I could stand. Certainly not a "meal." That would involve the maximum effort of chewing and digesting.

I reclined on the bed, arms outstretched, and looked at the ceiling. There is a hole up there made by a broom once when I was trying to kill a large waterbug. I didn't kill it. It had scuttled off with that creepy little sound they make when they run and hide. It left me alone with a dent in my ceiling. I sat back up. Things in life are inevitable. Our parents will die and roaches will always scurry into a crack, never to be squashed to death.

The last time I had sat in this room I was eighteen years old. I had a mother, two sets of grandparents, a sister, two uncles, an aunt by marriage, and one cousin. I was too young to understand my father's death, too far away to experience Poppy's. He died right before I moved to France. A bizarre feeling came over me. I had no parents. I just turned thirty-eight, my twenty-year high school reunion came and went recently, and I had no parents. Who would take care of me? Who would take care of me. It was absurd.

I must have sat there a really long time. I didn't notice the sun had started to go down. There were eerie shadows cast on the walls. Jake was at my feet. Granny D in the doorway. I was crying without any tears on my cheeks.

"Everyone dies, Faith," she said, quietly, taking a seat beside me.

"How can you say that?" I was angry without any rage showing through.

"I'm going to die, too." Calm.

"Oh, stop it!" Like a small tear in fabric, the rage was about to unravel.

"Your mom was ready to go."

"No one is ready to go!" Beary Gordy, my favorite stuffed bear, went sailing across the room when I swiped my hand over the dresser.

"She had a good life."

"No she didn't! She lived in this shit hole her entire life and did nothing!"

"She raised you girls."

"Oh, just shut up! Quit giving me this redundant, cliche crap to make me feel better." I pointed at myself. "Look at what I've done. She could have been more, and now, what does it matter?"

"She didn't want that, Faith. That's your life."

"I have a life. She didn't. She should have left this hick town."

"She liked it here. It was her home."

"It's not mine."

"This isn't about you, Faith." Granny D stood up. "You want me to tell you the truth?"

That got my attention.

"She was miserably lonely," she said, no remorse, no anger, no sadness. She said it matter-of-fact like it was something I should have known all along, obvious like the sky is blue. "All she wanted was for her girls to be here with her, but noooo. What were they off doing?" The anger was apparent now. Mine receded into a crack like a frightened bug. "One's off making fucking shi-shi foo-foo food in Boston. The other one's living in Hollywood, drawing animal designs on bed sheets. Neither of you could come home, could you? Too busy. Too busy."

"I didn't know."

"You didn't know? You didn't know what, Faith? That your mom was dying or that she wanted you here."

If I really were that bug, Granny D just shoved a broom into the crack and knocked off a leg.

She shook her head and walked out. "I'm going to bed. I microwaved you a plate. It's on the table."

Chapter 3

The spring in Arkansas is pleasant, everything blooms and the bees buzz about. The weather is warm and tolerable, but the summer is hot and muggy. Even in the early morning, my cup of coffee felt too hot going down. I wished for fall, cooler weather, brighter leaves. Heat or no, I still wished for a little breakfast. Granny D was frying up the ham from last night and making a side of eggs and buttered toast. No one can make buttered toast the way she can. I've tried, and I've been to Le Cordon Bleu. She layers the slice of bread evenly with butter then flips it onto the hot skillet, letting it sizzle just long enough to toast the edges and lightly brown the rest. It's greasy, buttery goodness, like a grilled cheese without the cheddar. If I were sleeping over at my grandparents, and I had a bad dream and couldn't sleep, she would get up and make me buttered skillet toast. Two o'clock in the morning and it didn't matter. She'd get up and do that for me.

I could smell breakfast cooking and couldn't resist it much

longer. From the screen door, I heard her say "Pops," which is what she called my grandfather. He's long dead but she still talks to him out loud. I *think* she knows he's not there, but I'm not sure. She told me he listens. Around her neck, she wears a gold heart pendant. The etching on the back reads: "Love, Poops." When Poppy D ordered the necklace for her, the engraver messed up, but my grandparents did not get mad. They thought it was the funniest thing, calling him "Poops" instead of "Pops." As a kid, my sister thought it was pretty funny, too. She even called him "Poopy D," but Mama thought that sounded bad.

"Is that a zit?" Granny asked, looking up from the skillet, as I came into the kitchen.

"What?" I touched my face. "No."

"It's a pimple," she said matter-of-fact. "Now get washed up."

My complexion was just fine.

I could smell the ham and my mouth watered. I had never gotten around to eating the night before. Part of me felt like I had dealt with Mama's death. I had gotten angry. That's what I was suppose to do, right? I felt sad. I could relax and eat. Everything would be fine. I could handle this.

In the bathroom, which was sickeningly painted in pale blue, I almost reached for the decorative soaps. You know the ones. Never to be used, little pink and blue roses that are like plastic fruit on a table. Unlike the fake fruit, these are actual cleansing bars trapped in their beauty, unable to be what they were born to be, like sad beauty queens. I also noticed that Granny had installed one of those bars in the bathtub to help her get in and out of the tub. I didn't know she was having trouble getting around. I asked her about it when I got back into the kitchen.

"The doctor said I should use that in case I fall. Told me to get one of them damned alert buttons you wear around your neck. Condescending prick, told me it was like a piece of jewelry," she said and served me a plate. "Like I'm too old to know what jewelry is." She tugged at her Poops necklace, knowingly, and fixed her own plate. She used Poppy D's favorite plate. He liked to eat out of the same one every meal. It was the last of the china from his mother's collection. It was probably a ridiculously expensive antique. There was a chip and a crack in one part, but Granny was always careful not to break it.

"Did you hear 'bout that car wreck in Little Rock? On those danged freeways. All those cars piled up on top of each other," she asked.

I didn't know what she was talking about. She probably saw it on the morning news. Before *Good Morning, America*, before *The Today Show*, there are local versions of a similar vein that air in Arkansas. They have "happy talk," give you the news, and teach you bizarre things like how to build your own barometer or the pros and cons of certain types of fertilizers. You can also win money. *Spinnin' 4 Winnings*, that's what it's called. Be ready for the phone to ring, they could call you. They flash a word on the screen and a certain amount of cash. At random, they ring you up, and if you know the word and amount, you win. Granny D waited for that call every damned day. She knew of people who had gotten "the call" and won big, you know, fifty bucks or so. With fifty bucks, you could buy a lot of crap at a garage sale, which are very big business on Saturdays. No one here really has a garage though. Very few homes are so lucky or so new. The signs tacked to the street lights usually say "Yard Sale," but they might say "Carport Sale" (some people do have those.) For the most part, it is just semantics. As they say, one person's trash, another person's treasure.

"We didn't have freeways in my day," she said, still on the wreck I knew nothing about. I think they did have freeways back then, but I didn't respond. "You like ham, right?" she asked. My grandmother's mind is like a blackberry, not the fruit, the electronic device. She has a large gigabyte of capacity to store information and likes to remind you of things. Problem is, she has a virus running through her and things sometimes get mixed up.

"I like ham," I said, chewing slowly. I wanted to smack it,

suck out the juice, but a proper, refined chef doesn't do such things.

"Is it your cousin Tootie who likes ham?"

"We both like ham. Uncle Henry doesn't eat ham. He converted to Judaism after he saw Madonna was into Kabbalah."

"Right, right." She saved and renamed the file: Uncle Henry, wears lipstick, no ham.

Uncle Henry, my dad's younger brother, is a transvestite. On weekends, he performs in a drag show out in Los Angeles as Madonna. He loves the 1980s Madonna with the bracelets and "boy toy" jewelry. I've never seen his show, but Gracie Ann says he's quite good. Growing up, he wasn't allowed to visit in drag. My mom thought it would confuse my sister and I. Womanly outfit aside, he looks nothing like my dad. My father sort of looked like a young Saint Nick, sans beard, but with rosy cheeks, curly blond hair, and a paunchy body that I am starting to inherit. I don't have many memories of him; my sister Gracie Ann has none. For the most part, from what Mama had told me, Dad was a fairly normal-type guy. That's not to say the Orions don't embrace the crazy; some of them just hide it better than others.

"Why'd they arrest you this time, Granny?" I asked, enjoying the ham.

She scoffed. "Oh. Thought I was drunk. Hauled me in for public intoxication."

"Were you drunk?"

She shifted, uneasy. My grandmother never felt uncomfortable. She looked around, sucked her teeth, then said, "I was doing a jig."

"A jig?"

"A jig." She waved her hands to explain. "A dance. Got it from Eddie. A Native American mourning dance."

"Uh huh. Eddie Field?"

She nodded.

"That man's still alive? He has to ..."

"Of course he's still alive. You graduated with him."

I almost choked on my food from laughter. "*Eddie* Field? I thought you meant his grandfather, Edward. What? Why was he teaching you Indian dances?"

"He knows things."

"Uh huh."

"I need you to go down there today." She got up and wrote out a list.

In school, Eddie Field was pale and gaunt, had scraggly brown hair with locks that curled around his ears, and always wore faded jeans, a punk rock T-shirt, and a pair of worn-out boots with gold-tipped toes and a chain around the ankle. He was the type of guy who would ditch class to smoke weed in the bathroom. Not exactly my clique. Of course Eddie Field became a mechanic. Typical.

She handed me the list. "Go by Maude's too. I need a few things. Take your mama's car. It's out back."

Mama drove a 1980 Mercedes she bought used in 1985. When I started making a lot of money, Mama still wouldn't let me buy her a new one. I looked outside. The odometer probably said something like three million miles. It is red, still has a "Vote Clinton" bumper sticker on the back, and a faded Domino's Pizza "Noid" doll in the rear window.

Granny D kissed me on the forehead, all grandmother-like, and took out money from her purse. "Get yourself anything you want, honey."

"Granny, I have cash."

Maude's grocery store only takes cash. Asking ol' Maude to figure out a credit card machine would be like asking a supermodel to comprehend the work of Stephen Hawking. It can't be done and no sense trying.

Granny D pursed her lips, holding out the cash. I didn't argue, planning to slip the money back into her wallet later.

"Most of this is stuff your sister wants," she said.

My sister, her husband, and their three kids were coming in

later. Whenever they arrived anywhere, they came in like a caravan of circus people – colorful, strange, and a little creepy. They were flying in and renting a car. L.A. people. Forget about a train. That's, like totally, public transportation! My sister is thin as a reed, wears big red glasses like Sally Jessy Raphael, and has wavy blond hair that is straight out of Hollywood. She's three years younger than me and designs bed sheets. Working as a graphic designer, she had her first success with a set of sheets covered in yellow hippos. Now she has her own company, Art Sheets. We've always gotten along, even though part of us is diametrically opposed. We both wanted to get out of Mulberry Field, but her mental thread count is a little low, believing in everything mystical. New age trends blow in and out of her life like a breeze. It is funny though that she once had a "vision" of marrying Walt Disney. Her husband looks just like him. He has a little mustache, hair combed into some 1950s style, and directs B-movies. His films always have names like *Flying Bugs from Zombie Land* and star strange celebrities that everyone knows but no one knows why they are famous. They certainly aren't getting much attention from starring in a Glen "Jonesy" Jones Production. Jonesy thinks of himself as something of an auteur; he writes, directs, produces, and sometimes stars in his own films. Problem is, they are all crap. Real, utter shit. Like Lucy to Ricky Ricardo, he bugs me about being on my show. He has this grand idea, since he's a "celebrity," for me to have a "cooking with the stars" segment and feature him. Geez. I'd rather cook with someone in a Mickey Mouse costume.

Luckily, all three of Gracie Ann's girls look like their mother. The identical twins, age twelve, are named Starry and Night. They aren't big fans of Van Gogh. The kids were conceived on a star-filled evening in the back of a pick-up truck on Mulholland Drive in Hollywood. They don't live far from the conception site, actually. They have a fairly nice Tudor-style home on Laurel Canyon near Jim Morrison's old house. Their six-year-old, Lucy, got a normal first name, but her middle name is Bes without the extra letter "S," named after the

Egyptian god who wards off evil spirits during childbirth. Lucy must have been protected by more than one god, because she came out as sweet as a good pitcher of tea. Like her sisters, her conception is worth a mention. Gracie Ann had a dream about the Egyptian goddess Isis holding the hand of a little girl. Being that our last name is Orion, Gracie Ann has a "thing" with the constellation, which in Egyptian myth correlates with Osiris and Isis. The three great Egyptian pyramids on the Giza Plateau are aligned with Orion's belt. In Gracie Ann's opinion, the stars were aligned perfectly over the Hollywood Hills, and the dream was a sign to have another child, so out popped Lucy. Gracie Ann swears she looks just like the kid from the dream. Dream or no, I adore Lucy. She could have been my daughter. She eats gracefully, wears pink slippers because she wants to be a dancer, and writes me one fan letter a week just in case I don't get any. She's a real peach. A real goddess.

I looked over Granny D's grocery list. Gracie Ann wanted a pineapple and her girls requested Fizz, a terrible soft drink made of carbonated water, peach juice, and milk. I wasn't sure Maude would have Fizz, so I'd probably end up in Safeway too. Gracie Ann likes her kids to eat healthy, but when they come out here, that usually goes out the window. If your fingers aren't oily after a meal here, then you skipped food altogether and only drank iced tea. Granny D's sweet tea is like her buttered skillet toast. Nothing like a snowflake, it is consistently the same. Always good.

I checked my bobbed hair in my compact mirror and nodded to Granny D. "I'll be back before Gracie Ann gets here." I hoped that would turn out to be a lie.

"Don't forget to tell Eddie to get his butt down here this afternoon before your sister arrives, too. I want my fridge fully operational!" She yelled the last part to me as I walked out the back door into the hot, mulberry-scented air.

Chapter 4

Eddie Field is a third generation Edward Field, second generation mechanic. His father ran off when Eddie was a baby to join a rock band. Eddie's mother died in childbirth and was pale as snow with Scottish ancestry and red hair. The Field family are full-blooded Cherokee Indian. They started as the "Fields" family until Eddie's great-grandfather bought seven acres in Mulberry, cleared the land, and chopped off the letter "S" from the name, thinking it would look better like a bulldog with a stubby tail. The last I remembered it had one trailer on a spot of barren wasteland. A couple of pines, a picnic table, a motorcycle, a used car, and various junk were the only things I ever remembered seeing in Eddie's unkempt yard. Technically, he's our neighbor, but the properties are so spread out that you would get winded walking over to borrow a cup of sugar.

When I got to the garage, which is near the strip mall, Edward Sr., a sack of skin and bones, greeted me with a warm hug. He smelled like bacon fat, had a skull earring in one ear, and a tattoo of a wave over his left eye.

"Your granny doing a'right?"

"Yes, sir."

"Sorry to hear 'bout your mama."

He pulled a flat, polished stone out of his pant's pocket and placed it gently in my palm, closing my fingers around it. "It'll make you feel better," he said and tottered off, making a jingling noise as he walked.

The Fields embrace the crazy too. Back in the day, Edward Sr. was a legend just like Granny D. She worked her magic in the kitchen, he in the garage. It wasn't German engineering that had kept Mama's car running all those years. It was Edward Sr. Now he muttered things to himself sitting outside on a bench with a cigarette.

The small garage hadn't changed in years. It still had two work stations, both presently filled with a car up on blocks and some guys puttering around, and two offices. The front office was for customers with a waiting area and the usual assortment of items for sale (cigarettes, Cokes, gum). The back room was for managing the establishment. In high school, it was also the rumored location of many a girl's lost virginity by motorcycle-ridin', greasy-haired Eddie Jr. He never took a girl to a dance. You wouldn't catch him hanging out at IHOP in Little Rock with a date. No one entwined her fingers in his as he lackadaisically perused the school hallways. Yet, he managed to have, allegedly, deflowered half the graduating class. I steered clear of him.

Somewhere in the garage, echoing off the cement walls, I heard a deep, calm voice say, "It won't move forward. I can't figure it out." Then that same voice was behind me. "Faith Orion, as I live and breathe," he said. I looked up from examining an expired Reeses cup and right into dark green eyes, the color of a rich pine forest. With high cheek bones and a sideways grin that looked near-smirk, Eddie Field deserved to be on the cover of a magazine like an A-list actor.

You always have an image of a high school classmate etched in your mind. Forever young like a painting. When you see them again years later it is always unsettling. Things have shifted and moved, weight has been put on or taken off, hairstyles have changed, but they look the same. Although young and vibrant, Eddie was no different, but I felt as if I had never really looked at that painting before. I took him all in now. Tall and thin, his jeans were tight, his belt worn leather, and his shoes ragged green work boots – without the gold tips or chain from high school. Over an oil-stained T-shirt, he wore a short-sleeved shirt with the name "James" patched over the pocket. One wrist was covered in bracelets, the other with a red ribbon. I peered past him to the office in the back. I could see the naugahyde sofa that he had reclined many a teenage girl upon. A guitar rested on it.

Holding an oily car part in his hands, Eddie stared at me too. His lips are perfectly pursed like he is about to kiss you even though he is only staring without saying a word. He put the car part down, wiped his hands on a clean rag, and had this suspicious air about him that he didn't have when he first came into the office. Eddie remembered the image of me he had etched in his mind perfectly well. Valedictorian, prom queen, cheerleader. Famous chef. I didn't belong there. Our cliques still didn't click.

"I'm sorry about your mom." Genuine sympathy for Mama, but a cool voice for me. Not icy, but not friendly. His nearly shoulder-length dark hair was a little wavy from the humidity, and it fell into his eyes. He ran his fingers through it, and I noticed his hands looked very clean for a mechanic.

"We knew it was coming," I said in reference to Mama.

"Did you?" There was something about the way he said it that made me feel uncomfortable.

I cleared my throat. "I came for a part. Granny said you ordered it for her. For the tractor."

He motioned for me to come inside the office. It was small, smelled of cigarettes and a woodsy cologne. I thought it was Burberry, but I couldn't imagine him wearing something like that. He dug around some neatly piled boxes on the floor, then opened his desk drawer and rummaged again. His desk was tidy. Desk calendar, coffee mug, notepads. There was a fortune cookie slip tacked to his computer that read "Follow your inner moonlight; don't hide the madness" by Allen Ginsberg. There was a framed photo of a little boy with red hair, but no pictures of any women, not even a calendar of scantily-clad women on the walls. The more I looked around, the more my yearbook-inspired photo of Eddie began to change. There was a row of books on a hand-made shelf against one wall, a coloring book picture of Scooby Doo, and a vase of roses haphazardly leaning against the opposite wall on the floor. I stepped closer to the shelf and saw the authors: Mark Twain, Tennessee Williams, and James Joyce. There were books on Native American mysticism, books on quantum mechanics, and a few on astronomy.

"Here you go. She need any help installing it?" he said, finally finding the part and handing it to me. I saw the gold band on his left ring finger.

"Of course she needs help. She's eighty-four."

"I never want to offend her. Hell hath no fury like Granny D scorned."

This was true.

"She needs help with the fridge, too."

"What happened to the fridge?"

I shrugged. "It's dead." The word "dead" came out of my mouth like a shocking bite of soured beans. I couldn't wash out the flavor, clear my nostrils of the smell, or vanish the image of anything deceased from my head.

"She usually fixes everything," I said, but he noticed my discomfort.

"She can't this time." He nodded, pondered. He squinted his eyes, serious expression, but seemed to be thinking about more than busted refrigerators or grandmothers who can still plow a field. There was something philosophical on the tip of his tongue. Gracie Ann would call this a "sixth sense," but I didn't like the way he looked at me, probing, sure of himself.

"She asked Ol' man Wilson, Barney Wilson, to have a look. He couldn't get into it either," I said, trying to sound confident, not sad. "She thought he could, because he has small hands."

Eddie looked down at his hands. His serious expression slightly broken like water pushing through a block of ice. With almost a grin, he said, "That makes me feel good."

"No, no, I didn't mean that. I think you'll have to take the back off ... off the fridge. She can't get it off. The food's stored in the freezer and Gracie Ann's coming in ... "

"Gracie Ann," he interrupted with a full-on smile. "How's she?"

Gracie Ann had been one of the naugahyde couch's "reclinees."

"Married, three kids."

He nodded. "Yeah. I know that. I meant how is she handling the ... your mama's ... "

"As well as expected."

"Gracie Ann visits every holiday season. Brings me an apple-spiced Bundt cake from a shop on Melrose Avenue." He was genuinely charmed by the sentiment.

"Well, she's nice like that."

He gave me a hard stare and nodded cooly. "She's a sweet girl."

"I have to go."

I turned to walk out and he asked, "How come you don't feature any of your grandmother's recipes on your show?"

"I don't make those types of things on my show."

"She's a good cook." He nodded, then added, "I'll be over after lunch."

****

When I got to Maude's, I was thinking about how much I wanted to kick Eddie Field in the nuts. I *don't* make those types of foods on my show! I knew his insinuation. I know my grandmother is a good cook. It's not personal. I stomped around the store and looked for the items on Granny D's list. I make fine French cuisine. I received the Grand Diploma from Le Cordon Bleu. What did Eddie know about cooking? Peeved, I didn't take the time to notice how Maude's store had changed very little. Five aisles of groceries, fresh produce in the front, frozen goods in the back. Maude still ringing up customers. As a teenager, almost every day, I used to get a Mountain Dew and ice cream sandwich as my little after-school snack. Her grandson Damon always bugged me to go skating with him down at Willow Springs Park. He swept the floors back then and used to playfully nudge my feet with the broom. I didn't dislike him, but had no desire to put wheels on my feet and couple's skate with him. I did notice he was nowhere in the store now. I had heard he moved to Arizona, writes a sports column for the paper there.

I was still reeling when I got up to the register, but I was happy I found the Fizz and wouldn't have to go to Safeway. Maude gave me the obligatory "I'm so sorry about your mother" speech and kept asking me questions about lupus that I couldn't answer. Lost in her own thoughts, she didn't notice that her low-hanging boob got stuck in the grocery sack. It popped out when she picked up the bag and hit her square in the nose.

"Goodness," she exclaimed, rubbing her sunburned nose.

Her grandson Damon would have cackled had he seen that, but it wasn't funny to me. I still wanted to kick Eddie in the nuts. The nerve of him trying to suggest that I *should* feature any of Granny D's cooking on *my* show. Granny cooks "home style" food, fried and buttery and, well, good. It's just *not* what I do.

When I got home, Granny D was sitting on the back steps with Tag, a junk seller from Atlanta who still "runs moonshine" state to state. His age is questionable, but he has scraggly, sandy brown hair (probably some actual sand in it too) and looks like he drinks gasoline, which is what his 'shine tastes like. In his hand, he had a box of Granny's leftover jam jars – he fills them with the white lightning. Granny doesn't mind. She gets free whiskey that way, trading jars for liquor.

"Faith Orion," he said in the heaviest Southern accent a human being can have. "Lookit ya gurl! Done good, hell yeah! Big TV star!" He put the jars down and put his hands on my shoulders, took me all in.

"She's skin and bones," Granny said.

"Ya look very pretty, miss," he said, picking the jars back up. "Gotta make another run." He looked back at Granny. "Seen Edward Field 'round?"

"Yeah, he's probably at the garage," Granny answered, then turned to me. "Get my part?"

I nodded, although I still wanted to kick someone in the parts. Tag hobbled off, waved goodbye, and crawled into a beat-up, hippie-style van. As he drove in the direction of Edward Field's Auto Repair, the van backfired, running off white lightning.

I gave Granny the tractor part and carried the groceries inside.

"Let's have some lunch," she said.

We put away the groceries, then chowed down on a ham sandwich and chips. My mind was still on ways to smash Eddie's testicles when Granny mentioned his name again.

"Did you and Eddie get to catch up a bit?"

"Catch up on what?"

"High school stuff. Friends."

"He wasn't my friend."

"Oh. Gracie Ann likes him."

"Yeah." Annoyed.

"He's a nice boy."

"He was a screw up in high school who would never amount to anything and he didn't."

"Didn't amount to anything?" She huffed. "He runs his own

business, can fix anything, teaches kids on Saturdays at the community center, and plays guitar like a rock legend. Have you ever heard him play?"

"What? No. I don't ... how do you know he plays?"

"Down at the Whiskey Biskey. He plays every Saturday night with his band, Eddie Field and the Live Jive."

"You don't have any business going down to that dive."

"It's not a dive."

Indeed it is a dive. Right off the freeway before you hit the exit to Scott, it is the type of place with cheap beer, women wearing low-cut shirts, and a large parking lot in the back for truck drivers to snooze after whooping it up inside.

"What could Eddie possibly teach children down at the center?"

"What was it you studied at Princeton?"

"Harvard."

"Harvard. Princeton. Whatever. What was it?"

"English lit."

"That's what he teaches. Literature."

"Literature? He could barely pass English in school!"

Granny laughed ferociously. "Sure? People surprise you sometimes." She looked at me curiously. "You can't always judge people by the way they look, Faith."

"Why? He looks like he should be under the hood of someone's car and that's exactly what he does."

She cleaned her plate in the sink and shrugged. "Eh, under the hood of a car. Doesn't make him less of a person."

"I'm not saying that."

"What's the difference between making biscuits and making croissants?"

"None. I guess."

"What's the difference between fixing cars and designing them?"

"There's a big difference there."

"It's just a job. It's not a person, Faith."

If I didn't find some balls to smash, I was going to go insane. I looked down at Jake the dog. He had balls. Instinctively, his ears went up and he ran out of the kitchen. Arms crossed, I snorted.

Chapter 5

Most people are inefficient at trying to calm a fury-raged
Granny D. Eddie took the don't-try-at-all approach. It wasn't effec-
tive. A salt shaker went flying. He looked at me. I was smug.

"You might as well go out and pull me a switch if you tell me
my fridge can't be fixed," she stormed.

Calmly, Eddie walked out the back door and returned with a
long twig, stripped and ready to go. He handed it to her. "Your fridge
can't be fixed," he said.

I think it was the first belly laugh I've had in years. Granny D
looked at me and put her hands on her hips. She wanted to laugh too.

"Someone's taking me to Sears," she said and pointed at me.
"You?" Granny D's license had been revoked years ago for reckless
driving. She turned to Eddie. "You. You have a truck. You're taking
me to Sears."

Moments later the three of us headed to the Sears in Little
Rock. The city is an hour and a half drive from Mulberry Field. The

Sears is on University Avenue, along with the IHOP, and the street is much the same as it was in my high school days too. There is the hospital, the college, and a couple of malls. It used to be one of the main drags, but most people have moved farther west now. West Little Rock is almost a city in itself, like West Hollywood. The people are keen to point out that they live in "west" Little Rock, not south, not North (which is actually a city), and certainly, for the love of all that's good, not *east*. The West Little Rockers all go to big churches, think they have plenty of money, and shop every Saturday at Barnes & Noble, Target, and Linens 'n Things. The intellectuals, who wish they lived in Soho or the Village in New York, reside in the refurbished downtown with the lofts, coffee shops, and nightclubs. On Saturdays they check out books in the main library, skipping BN, and buy produce at the farmer's market. Most of them have never been to Los Angeles, New York, or Chicago. They try hard to imagine they aren't in the South, and Little Rock tries very hard to be a big city.

We jetted along the fast-moving freeway, past the airport, past the capitol building that looks like the nation's capitol, and past everything I remembered from my youth. I realized that Little Rock is one of the cleanest cities I've ever been in. You don't see graffiti on the walls, and the streets and sidewalks are nearly litter-free. Tourist can stroll the streets without much worry of being mugged as they snap pictures of the Clinton Presidential Library or the home used in *Designing Women*. They marvel at the charming accents and ask people if they've ever met former residents Mary Steenburgen, Billy Bob Thornton, or me. Unlike those two actors, I have always kept my upbringing low key, even losing my Southern accent. But they do know me here. No one forgets. Being Southern is like having maple syrup poured all over you; it just sticks. You can never get it completely off no matter how many hot baths you take.

Even though I hadn't been home in twenty years, I knew we were coming up on the University exit. Sitting next to Eddie, I tried to guess what cologne he was wearing. He certainly didn't smell the way a mechanic should. I had to respect the way he had dealt with Granny, and my desire to knee his groin was waning. Tom Petty's *Down South* played from a CD; Granny bopped along, let her hand make a wave motion as she stuck it out the window. Eddie kept his CDs in a little holder that was tacked to his visor. I wanted to take it down and look at it. Musical tastes say a lot about a person. As a teenager, I listened to the same thing as everyone else in the 1980s, Bruce Springsteen, Michael Jackson, The Go-Go's. I still like those tunes, but my tastes are more cultured. I like jazz, classical, opera. Gracie Ann listens to a lot of new age, stuff like Andreas Vollenweider and Yanni, but she's still a rocker at heart. Granny D likes everything. See, Poppy D started out as a musician. That's how they met. He played slide trombone in a swing band at some speakeasy on the corner of 65th and Arch Street. Granny D tells the story of how she saw him in a brown fedora, sun-glasses, and a hep, bronze-colored suit. He was carrying his trombone, winked at Granny D, and after she heard him play, she let him take her for a ride in the sidecar of his motorcycle. It's funny to imagine my grandparents as young people riding around Little Rock in that antique contraption. He had a special talent in making drop biscuits, too. The spikey-looking biscuits are so named because they are literally dropped off the spoon and onto the pan, making various shapes with small bumps. To combine the drop biscuits with Granny D's mulberry jam was the perfect idea. They could go into business together, but Poppy D had another idea too. After several shots of whiskey, he peed on the sidewalk and asked her to marry him.

Poppy D died right before I started Le Cordon Bleu. Gracie Ann was about to start college at USC, and the family had planned to visit me before my big move to Europe. Gracie Ann and Mama did visit me before I left, not long after the funeral, but Granny couldn't make it. She was still waiting on her "sign" from Poppy. Signs are a big thing in my family. They can come in any shape or form as long as they have some personal significance. Gracie Ann reads license plates. Whenever she needs an answer, she asks "the universe" for a sign on the next personalized license plate she sees. The Department of Motor Vehicles did not play any role in Granny D's sign though. She eventually got her sign in the form of a yellow flower. "That ol' Pops," Granny had told Mama via telephone at my dorm, "sprouted a yellow flower out by the tire swing." Yellow is Granny D's favorite color. Granny is also nuts.

After Poppy's death, Granny D stopped giving out a bag of drop biscuits with each jar of jam. She claimed she could never get the drop biscuits to come out near as good. "I always burn the butts," she has said, but I think it breaks her heart to make them. She has adjusted fairly well to life without her husband, in much the same way that I have. We've been divorced for three years now. Even though I did love Stephan at one time, I don't think I ever believed in "til death do us part." I could never imagine growing old with him. Granny and Poppy could sit on the porch together for hours without saying a word, then instinctively know the other wanted a glass of lemonade or a sandwich. Stephan and I never had that. We didn't hold hands. We didn't frolic giddy-like in public. We were a good team though. We married after I finished Le Cordon Bleu and lived in France for awhile until we moved to New York. I had a great job as a head chef at a restaurant; Stephan freelanced as a food critic. Before long, Stephan's articles were so popular that he published his first book. Through a mutual friend, I heard about a new network that featured cooking shows, and I auditioned to get a gig. They didn't think I had enough experience for my own show, so I took a job in Boston instead, not far from my old Harvard dorm. My road to celebrity-hood started when Stephan's literary agent tasted my cuisine. By the time I was thirty, I had three successful cookbooks, and the FoodWorks Channel called me.

The FWC has kept me busy for the past eight years. My contract requires me to do two live holiday specials every year, Thanksgiving and Christmas. Everyone comes home for the holidays in my family, and they made watching my specials part of the routine, part of the traditions, since I can't be there. Gracie Ann and her brood are the only ones I see often. There are FoodWorks studios in Los Angeles, and I tape shows there sometimes. Aside from that, I've stayed in Boston. Last year I spent Christmas with my ex-boyfriend Teddy; he's a weatherman who is short and wears a girdle. We broke up when a new anchor joined his station and he started seeing her. In Mulberry Field, the choices for mates are even slimmer. Gracie Ann believes in soulmates, but like I said, the idea of "til death do us part" was a scary concept for me.

I looked over at Eddie as we took the University exit. His hair wasn't greasy. Why had I ever thought that? It looked soft. He wasn't wearing the overshirt with the name "James" from earlier in the day, just his T-shirt, and I saw the same name was tattooed on his right arm. I looked at a photo of a little red-haired boy hanging from the rearview mirror, the same kid in the picture in Eddie's office.

"Who's James?" I asked.

He looked down at his tattoo, tapped the photo, and said, "My son. He's eight."

I looked at his left hand. The ring. Granny noticed my glance, got a mischievous look on her face. "How is Janet?"

He nodded. "She's great. Yeah."

I was glad to see the big, square building with the word "SEARS" written across it. Eddie pulled in, parked, and we went inside. Granny was on the prowl for a Kenmore. Sears brand, that's quality. Forget Maytag and their never-used repairman. Granny D and Poppy D swore by Kenmore. Eddie Field probably wasn't quality either, even if he did have silky hair. He had a family and it didn't need repair.

Chapter 6

The circus was in town when we pulled into the driveway. There was a white SUV next to Mama's car. Granny D had left the key under the mat in case they arrived before we got back. Gracie Ann, hearing the truck pull up, came out onto the steps, eating an ice cream sandwich. She was into my stash.

"I thought that was your truck," Gracie Ann said to Eddie as he got out. He picked her up and spun her around. Her husband, you know, the Walt Disney lookalike, came out onto the steps, smoking a pipe, and didn't even flinch, even though Gracie Ann had her legs kicked up like a teenager being swung around by her boyfriend. Eddie put her down and she kissed him ever so gently on the lips. Eddie whispered into her ear, but I was standing near enough them to hear. He said, "I'm sorry."

Gracie Ann nodded. "Thank you." Her voice was soft for a moment, and then back to her old self. She looked at me and said, "Hey ya."

"Hey ya, back at ya," I replied, our customary way of greeting one another.

As if on a friendly visit, ready to playfully insult her older sister, she jabbed, "You look thinner on TV. I thought television added ten pounds?"

Granny D chimed in with a huff. "She's skin and bones."

"Nice tan," I said, coming up with my own sisterly jab. "Did it come out of a bottle?"

"Sprayed on, nice and orange, ain't it?" We both laughed. "You aren't going to give me a hug? That's bad karma," Gracie Ann said, grabbing me for a bear hug. She squeezed Granny D, then motioned for her husband Jonesy to say hello to Eddie.

Jonesy is always excited, always happy, always a little ... much. "Hot tamales and get your lemons!" he yelled when he saw Eddie. The origin of his catch phrase about tamales and lemons is unknown, but I do know that he signs autographs that way. "Eddie, my friend! Good to see you, good to see you!" He hugged Eddie, patted him on the back roughly the way men do.

"Want to give me a hand with this?" Eddie asked him, referring to the refrigerator in the back of the truck.

"Absolutely!" Jonesy tapped out his pipe, took off his jacket, and rolled up his 1950s-style shirt sleeves. Ever the optimist and extroverted, he is always ready to be part of the action. He fits right in with my "embrace the crazy" family. Jonesy loves pulling a watermelon out of the garden, slicing it open with a pocket knife, and eating it right there in the field, dirty hands and all. Very different from Wee Ste-fan.

"That's a big fridge. Really big. Yeah. Store a lot of goodies in there, eh, Tomato Puddin'?" Jonesy said to Gracie Ann. Like his tamale and lemon catch phrase, I do not know why he calls my sister Tomato Puddin'. I do not ask.

Before they could get to work moving the refrigerator, Lucy bounded down the steps. She was in all pink and looked adorable as always. Her twin sisters slowly made their way out, lazy and with the same sprayed-on tan as their mother. There is only one physical way to tell the twins apart – Starry has pierced ears – but talk to them long enough and you see blatant personality differences.

"Aunt Faith!" Lucy yelled. Being raised in Los Angeles, Jonesy and the girls don't have Southern accents. Mine disappeared with the help of a voice coach and living in France for so long. Lucy hugged me and I spun her around the same way that Eddie had done Gracie Ann. I put her down and asked, "Did you get an ice cream sandwich too?"

She looked at me, serious, and said, "My grandma is dead." Then she did what all of us had been avoiding. She wept openly. It wasn't a dam bursting; it was a hurricane. As hard as she could, she jumped up and down, getting her pink shoes all dirty, and screamed repeatedly, "I want her back right now!" With all the rage of a volcano, the little six-year-old looked at Eddie then at his truck. A moment of silence. Lucy kicked in his right headlight. She only had the chance to hop around in pain once before Eddie snatched her up and sat her on the hood of the truck. He looked down at her foot; Jonesy checked it out too. Gracie Ann stood there like an ice sculpture.

Eddie took off the ribbon from his wrist and tied it on Lucy's wrist. He whispered something in her ear.

"Really?" she said, only whimpering a little now.

He nodded and smiled.

She hopped off the car. Her foot was fine. "Really really?"

"Mmmhmmm," he said.

Granny D took her by the hand and went up the steps. "You ever had a milk popsicle?" Granny asked her. Lucy shook her head. "Me either. Let's chop off a piece from the milk block in the freezer and see how it is. Come on girls," Granny D said to the twins, then turned back to look at the rest of us. "I want my fridge! Get a move on!" They went inside; we surveyed the hurricane damage.

"Wow! Firecracker, she is. I'll pay for that," Jonesy said, looking at the broken headlight and shaking his head with the same excited expression he always has on his face.

"I can fix it. Don't worry about it. I've got stuff around the shop. Won't take me ten minutes to repair it."

As if suddenly waking up to the smell of smoke in the house, concerned and afraid, Gracie Ann was alert again and looked at me. "Have you been up to the house yet?" she asked.

"No."

"Wanna go?"

"No."

On her own, she turned and walked down the driveway/road up to our house. The guys went to work unloading the refrigerator, and I saw Gracie Ann break out into a run.

****

Our old house looks completely different than Granny D's. Granny's house is country-style, yellow clapboard with green shutters; it looks like a doll house. Our home is red brick, chimney, with a garage. It could just as easily have been in the suburbs. It doesn't really belong on this dusty, dirt road that is really a driveway. Just like Mama. She looks – looked, I have to remember to talk in past tense now – like a dame from a Fellini film. Dark hair, dark eyes, pressed clothes, and wide-brimmed hat. She was all film noir without knowing it. My friends always said she looked "glamorous." They didn't know she wore the hats to keep the sun off her skin because of her lupus. They didn't know that I secretly resented her for being so beautiful, being so smart, and settling for being a mother. Mama could have been a model. Mama could have been a doctor. But Mama met Dad and became Mom.

When I stepped into our house, nothing had changed – the same pictures on the walls, the same sofa, the same smells. Gracie Ann was sitting on the couch and she looked at me with red, wet eyes. I knew it was for Mama, but she has stared at me with those tear-filled eyes many times before. She's the emotional weepy type, whether it be for sadness or joy.

"Hey ya," she said.

"Hey ya, back at ya."

"Are you going to sleep here?"

I shook my head.

"Glen and I usually sleep at Granny's, the girls here with Mama. There's not enough room at Granny's, if you're in the old room," she said. "I guess Lucy can have your room, the girls mine, and Glen and I can sleep in Mama's room." She paused at her words. "Did you hear that? My husband and I in Mama's room. The girls in our old rooms." Perplexed. "I'm the parent now."

"You've been a parent a long time."

"Yeah, but it feels for real now."

I didn't want to say it but I did. "We don't have parents, Gracie. That's what hit me." I sat down beside her. "Is that selfish? Is it childish?"

"We can't be childish. We're adults."

"We've been adults for a long time, too."

"It feels different."

Different. I've struggled for that my whole life. Something different here. Something not like my family. My own unique identity. Adulthood was something I craved for as far back as I can remember. I'm not one of those people who looks back on childhood, wishing I could return. Aside from twirling on a tire swing, I never wanted childish things. I never liked them. I wanted to cook with Granny D or help Mama with errands. Gracie Ann liked being a kid. She played dolls, got dirty in the mud, and spent hours exploring the woods. Now, all either of us wanted was our mommy.

"You never dealt with Poppy's death," Gracie Ann said, flicking through an old magazine on the coffee table. I could see the date, one year ago.

"I did."

"You didn't. You didn't even come home. You avoided it."

"I was about to move to France."

"I was about to move to California."

"I didn't have any money."

"Granny was going to send it to you."

"She's old. She needed it more than me."

Gracie Ann stood up and said, "You avoid things. You've always been like that." I didn't want to hear lies. She took a crystal necklace from around her neck and handed it to me. "Here. It'll make you feel better." Another rock. Just what I needed.

"Eddie's grandfather already gave me a shiny rock. I'm all stocked on shiny stones."

"Be a smart ass. I was just trying to help." She put the necklace back on.

"No, Gracie, you aren't. You're avoiding it too with that ridiculous new age crap."

"It's not crap."

"What's a rock going to bring me, Gracie? What? It's silly."

"It's something. Better than nothing. It'll make you feel better if you let it."

"Please." I paused a moment. "Eddie's just as bad as you, giving Lucy that ribbon. Okay, it made her feel better, but it's not going to change anything."

"She's a child!"

"And so are you!"

"So."

"Mama's dead," I said, getting another taste of the soured beans. "Talk about me when you can't even say *that,* can you? You'll just look into your crystal ball and see that she's floating around in another dimension, the ether, heaven, whatever, and go back to drawing hippos on bed sheets. You weren't here for Mama."

"What? I come home every Christmas. Look at you, one ounce of fame, and you act like you're too good to come home for the holidays." Words really do sting worse than bees.

"I have a show to do!"

"Uh huh. In the beginning, yes, but you have clout at the station now. You can change that contract, tape the holiday specials. You tape plenty of specials."

"You weren't here for Mama anymore than me."

"Bullshit."

"Granny D said Mama wanted us here ... right before she passed." I could not say "died" this time.

"I was here," she replied, uncomfortable, wringing her hands. "I astral projected in."

I rolled my eyes. "You're out of your gourd!"

Astral projecting is like an out-of-body experience, except you don't pass away. During a deep meditative state, you "pretend" to float to other places. The idea is that you can see in detail various people, places, and events without leaving the comfort of your house. Kind of like watching live television without commercials.

"I was in a meditation, right before she died, like I knew it was coming without being there." Tear-filled eyes looked at me. "I saw her, Faith. Granny D was rubbing her forehead. Eddie was there too."

"Why was he there?"

She ignored my question like it was irrelevant. "She couldn't breathe." Gracie Ann looked at me, eyes wide, mouth open, her breathing heavy. Hocus pocus or not, her experience felt real to her. "Then she just stopped. Stopped breathing. I've never seen anyone die." Gracie Ann looked surprised, confused, and sad. "Their eyes stay open. Did you know that?"

I nodded, put my arm around her. "Gracie, it was just your imagination. You didn't really see Mama die."

"I did. That ribbon Eddie gave Lucy was Mama's."

"What?"

"It's from one of Mama's hats. I saw her give it to him before she died." The tears came out of her so fast, rivers flowing out of control, her lips shaking like the very trees grasping to remain on land during the flood. "She said ... " Gracie Ann could barely speak. "She said ... exactly this, 'Lucy will need it when she hurts her foot'."

You know how you feel when you watch a magic show and spend all your time trying to figure out the trick? That's how I felt at this moment; however, I could rationalize no trap door, no hidden mirrors, and no false compartment.

"It's probably just a coincidence." It was the best line I could think of.

She wiped her tears. "Maybe," she said for my benefit and smiled a little. "I know you think I believe a lot of weird things, and I don't always believe it either, but this, that moment, I know one hundred percent. I saw Mama die."

Gracie Ann was able to swallow the soured beans whole, not chewing, and let the nasty taste do its worst to her. She saw Mama die. Die. Mama's dead. Mama's Dead. My stomach churned. I threw up all over the coffee table.

Chapter 7

I woke to the taste of bile in my throat, the smell of sausage cooking in the kitchen. When I had returned back to Granny D's, Eddie and Jonesy had the fridge installed. I had ignored everyone, went to my room, and never came back out. The thought of Mama being dead sat in my mind like grease floating around in a wet pan. It left its oily residue everywhere. It was like Vaseline smeared on the wall. You can wipe it off but there will always be a stain.

Even though I hadn't been home in twenty years, the last time I saw Mama was a visit she made to Boston after Stephan left me. Even though she embraced the crazy just as much as anyone else in my family, she was acceptable to introduce to my FWC family. Like I said, Mama looked like a black-n-white movie queen. She was Bergman in *Casablanca*, forever classic, classy to anyone she meets. Raven-colored hair like Elizabeth Taylor, a sweet face like Sally Field, and the demeanor of Grace Kelly. I enjoyed having her in Boston, showing her all I had become. I still had some of the smugness – I wanted to show off – but part of me wanted her to share in my famous world, my famous life. Couldn't she see how much better it was like that? I didn't need a husband or children. Famous chef! We had sat up late one night watching *Citizen Kane*. Too much wine and I start acting silly, which I did, mimicking the deep voice of Orson Welles. Like a drunk being sobered up with a slap in the face, Mama had said, "I worry you'll end up like that."

"Like Charles Foster Kane?" I had exclaimed, nearly dropping a plate of food.

"You take a lot of pride in shallow things. I don't want you to end up alone or lonely."

"Is this about Stephan? He found a skinny whore he liked better. Big deal. I'm fine, Mama."

"No, you're not, and this isn't about Stephan. It's about you. Nothing here is real. It's a beautiful smile. A beautiful setting. Everything is as perfect as a picture in a high-gloss magazine, all the airbrushing, all the retouching, but it's not the truth, is it, Faith?"

"I have more than you ever had."

"Do you? Your life is like plastic fruit. It looks pretty, but it can't nourish you."

"Fuck you, Mother." Mom looked away. It was hateful. I knew it.

"Your world here, it's fantasy. You avoid reality," she replied.

"I'm the only one in this family rooted in reality. I never 'embrace the crazy' like the rest of you."

"You don't even know what that means," she had said back. "That's what worries me."

I didn't know what she meant by that. Lying in bed now, no longer able to hear her voice, that comment and everything she had ever said to me, advice, loving words, scoldings, all screamed in my head like loud children at a playground. I'd hone in on one voice, see what it was saying, listen to it until I felt like crying, then tap into another comment and laugh just the same.

Listening to voices in your head is a sign of craziness. I got up, took a shower, and walked into the kitchen, calm, refined, the picture of polished elegance. They were all there – Granny D, Gracie Ann, Jonesy, and the three girls. I nodded a polite "Good morning" and went to the new refrigerator. They said nothing and continued to stuff their faces with sausage. I took out a grapefruit, sliced it open, sat down, and ate with a napkin in my lap and spoon in my hand.

"Can I have grapefruit like Aunt Faith?" Lucy asked. She had on a cute little pink hat and a candy bracelet, the kind that look neat but do not taste very good. Gracie Ann nodded, and I got up and put the other half on a plate for Lucy. She mimicked the way that I ate, slowly, keeping her elbows off the table.

Aside from small talk, everyone kept fairly quiet, even Granny D. Uncle John and Aunt Jane would be there by noon. They had a room at the Holiday Inn on Geyer Springs in Little Rock. Geyer Springs used to be the main hangout when I was a teen. You cruised it. That's pretty much it – you cruised it – the turn-around point being McDonald's which is long since gone. Also gone are Uncle John's wild days. He's a born-again Christian now, but in his twenties he spent time at Cummins State Penitentiary for running a chop shop in Pine Bluff. I'm surprised he went to jail; Granny D said he was always able to worm his way out of situations. "He's as slippery as a greased turkey," she had said, which is far worse, you can imagine, than a greased pig. When he was a boy, he would run around the house, Granny D after him with a switch for some offensive he had done, but she could never catch him. Eventually, the police did. He manages a Western Grillin' now in Bentonville; his wife Jane works as a paper-pusher at Wal-Mart headquarters. Their daughter, Tootie, who's real name is Joanne, is thirty and lives in Oklahoma City, working as a dancer, but everyone knows she's a stripper. She was set to arrive that night and planned to stay with a friend in Scott. My dad's brother, Henry, was also coming in that night and renting a room at the Peabody Hotel in downtown Little Rock. The Peabody is famous in Memphis for having a row of ducks walk through the lobby on a red carpet once a day. The tradition continues at the L.R. establishment. Uncle Henry used to have a pet duck, and he would bring it in a little pink cat carrier whenever he came to visit. Billy was its name. Billy the Duck. Granny D always wanted to eat him. "He's a fat one, he is," she used to say, eyeing it with a watering mouth. I can't eat ducks to this day. I loved Billy the Duck.

Granny stood up and cleared the table. "I watched *Spinnin' 4 Winnings* this morning and some old coot won one hundred and twenty-five big ones."

"Isn't that something," Gracie Ann said, going over to the phone. "Lucy, do you want to play with James today?"

"Yes! I want to play with James!" she exclaimed, then quieted down and clasped her hands in her lap like a lady. "I brought my favorite DVD. We can watch it."

"Can we go for a walk?" Starry asked. She smokes. I could tell by her raspy voice. Not sure if her parents have ever noticed, but it was obvious to me.

Her sister, Night, rolled her eyes, then chimed in, "It's too muggy. The air is so sticky here. I don't want to go for a walk." Different voice. "I want to stay inside and do something."

"Walking's good for you, isn't that right, Tomato Puddin'?"

"It is," Gracie Ann answered, dialing Eddie's number. "Good exercise."

"Night, go with your sister and don't go too far," Jonesy said, lighting up his pipe.

Starry jumped up like any preteen escaping grown-ups. She was ready to get out and about, up to no good, no doubt. Annoyed, Night followed.

Gracie Ann talked to Eddie; he would bring James over later. Granny D turned to Lucy and said, "Honey, James will be over in a bit. Why don't you take your grapefruit into the living room and watch some television." Lucy picked up her plate, dainty-like, and carried it into the other room, then Granny got down to business. The funeral was the next day. Mama's. The grapefruit tasted sour now, and I pushed mine away. Granny D gave out orders like we were planning a military maneuver.

"Faith, you'll help with the cooking and none of that shi-shi food. Real food. I need to make another trip to Safeway. There won't be enough." She paused for only a moment. Everyone has to breathe, even Granny D. "Funeral downtown eight o'clock, grave site services at Ironton Cemetery, and reception after at the house. Got it?"

"Granny, did you plan all this by yourself?" I asked. Gracie Ann cleared her throat.

"You think I can't plan a funeral? I've planned plenty."

Gracie Ann and I looked at each other. I felt she wanted to tell me something, but so far the funeral sounded normal, nothing weird planned.

"We start cooking tonight!" Granny D said and stood, triumphant.

****

On the road to Safeway, Granny D and I picked up Night. She was walking alone. No Starry in sight like Vincent van Gogh's painting split in two.

"What the hell? Where's your sister?" Granny asked.

Night shrugged and said in that lazy teenage voice, "I don't know."

"Like hell you don't. Start talkin' or I'll bend your lil' butt over the hood of this car and tan it. Faith, pull back over so I can pull me a switch."

Like a miracle, Night remembered exactly what happened to her sister. The three of us set off to Ruthie Weston's house. Ruthie is my grandmother's arch enemy. Ruthie makes strawberry preserves and sells them with corn muffins. She drives a big silver Cadillac, wears heavy eyeliner, and spends all her earnings on gladiolus. Her yard blooms like a freakin' green house.

The house was in full bloom when we arrived. There was Starry, sitting on the porch, sitting on the lap of sixteen-year-old Brian Weston, Ruthie's great-grandson. Night had already explained on the drive up that Starry and Brian met last Christmas and had kept in touch by text messaging. Night didn't trust him and told Granny about the marijuana he had given them last time.

"Twelve years old and smoking weed!" Granny had exclaimed, livid. "I wouldn't expect less from those Westons!"

I wouldn't either. His father was in prison for drug possession and used to sell weed out of his locker in high school. You would imagine he was best friends with Eddie, but looking back, I couldn't remember the two of them ever socializing.

One thing is certain, Dunleys and Westons don't socialize with each other. I knew this was going to get ugly, so I thought it best for Night and I to stay in the car. I kept my hand on the door handle, though, in case I needed to jump into the fracas, because it was going to be a fracas.

Looking like a scarecrow in some centuries-old blouse with ruffles sticking out the arms and around her neck, Ruthie came out onto the porch. "Get off my property, you old whore!" she yelled at Granny D.

"I've come for my great-grandbaby," Granny D said.

"She's yours?" Ruthie was pissed.

"Maw-maw," Brian said, trying to explain. Later, he would have to deal with his own fracas, and it would probably involve a lickin'. Granny and Ruthie might not see eye to eye, but they both knew which trees made the best switches.

"Get off my property, you old whore," Ruthie said again, but this time it was directed at Starry.

I opened the car door.

****

Everyone looked at us when we got to Safeway. A Norman Rockwell painting we were not. Much closer to a mixed-up Picasso.

Granny had a bruise over her left eye. My shirt pocket was torn off, and I had stuffed it haphazardly into my pant's pocket. Starry had accidentally gotten knocked off the porch and landed in the gladiolus, so she had bits of flower stuck to her clothes, along with a dirt-covered and hand-spanked butt. Night would have stayed fine, if she hadn't gotten out of the car and wailed on Brian for getting her sister high. Even for a Weston, he had some manners, apparently, and he wouldn't hit her back. She pounded on him until he cried. Then Starry had started pounding on her sister to leave her boyfriend alone. It all ended when I threatened to "call the law." In the South, you don't call the "police" or the "cops," you always call the "law." If I had said this in Boston, they would have thought I was threatening a lawsuit, which Granny D wasn't against either. When it comes to Westons, you do what you gotta do.

We made our way to the jams and jellies aisle to see if the rumor was true. Indeed it was. Weston's Preserves were on the shelves. The label looked almost identical to Granny D's labels.

"I'm getting me a lawyer," Granny D said in disgust. "She slept with someone to get this."

No one would want to sleep with that frayed-out toothpick.

"You know she doesn't even use fresh strawberries," Granny said loudly. Everyone in the aisle turned to look. Granny saw it as a political platform to preach her word. "She doesn't! Canned strawberries! You may as well buy this other mass-marketed horseshit!" She picked up a name brand jar and smashed it to the floor.

Her words fell on deaf ears this time, because after having turned to look, they noticed something else in the aisle. A celebrity. FoodWorks fans are everywhere. We are like the boy bands of the chef circuit. We even have a resident hunk – B.B. Knight. His blond hair is a wig, his teeth have been bonded so many times you could use them as casings for a nuclear bomb, and his buns, and I'm talking his buttocks here, are made of plastic. He wears a padded butt. Women around the nation ogle his prosthetic, plastic, polyurethane posterior.

I signed a few autographs, said hello to Ricky, who I went to school with and now cleans up the messes as they come in over the intercom – clean up on aisle three – things like that. Night and Starry, being from Hollywood and having a "director" for a father, were impressed with this moment of fame. They got over their disagreement, bonded in family pride.

Something bizarre happened between all of us when we got back to the car. Laughter. Insane, hysterical laughter. The kind of chuckling that begins with one snort and ripples over everyone like a giant yawn. One person does it and everyone follows. Starry started it and unleashed a wave that probably lasted twenty minutes or so. When we were able to wipe our eyes and sit up straight, we headed home, arriving with mounds of groceries and many stories to recount.

Chapter 8

When we got back from Safeway, Eddie was there, fixing Granny D's tractor. She went right up to him, still a little peeved from the day's adventures.

"What do you think you're doing?" she asked.

"A favor. I heard you'd be cooking all day and night, so I thought I'd pitch in," he said, wiping sweat from his forehead. "Let me help."

"A'right, but don't be comin' 'round here thinking I *need* help," she said and headed inside with the groceries. "Just because I needed help with the fridge, don't mean I can't do for myself."

He smiled at me, looked at my disheveled self. "I have to ask," he said. "Westons?"

"You don't want to know."

"That's what I love about you Dunleys, always up for a good fight," he said as I carried my stack of groceries up the steps. The girls had already gone indoors with Granny.

"There was no fight," I said back.

"Pow pow," he said, joking, punching the air with both fists. "There was a fight."

"No fight."

Very matter-of-fact, he said, "I saw Starry with the Weston boy last night." He went back to work on the tractor, and I went back down the steps.

"Why didn't you do something?" I asked.

"I did. They were at Mulberry Pointe making out." Up a little ways from Mulberry Pointe is an unused barnstormer's landing strip. For some reason, people go there to make out. I felt a little green thinking about Eddie up there, either making out with the "little wifey" or screwing around on her. He gave me no explanation of that and said, "I took them both home, helped her sneak in, because I didn't want Granny D to know."

"She got back out."

"They usually do." Before I got inside, he said, "Two people who don't seem to belong together always somehow manage to get together."

"Because people, especially kids, are foolish and make bad decisions," I said, my knowledge of relationships based on a handful of boyfriends and one husband. The groceries were starting to feel heavy in my arms.

"I'm just saying," he said, tinkering with something on the tractor, "you can feel things for people you'd least expect to be attracted to on the surface." He gave me no more than that and went back to work.

Back inside, I was happy to be relived of my grocery sacks, but Gracie Ann and Jonesy had their hands full in a completely different way. Starry got her punishment doled out. She had lied about her walk, smoked weed, and worst of all, been hanging with a Weston. I thought it was quite hypocritical for Gracie Ann to lay into her about the pot, though. Gracie Ann had smoked her fair share of weed growing up, but Starry was grounded for it just the same – no television or internet for a week when they got back to L.A. If Mama had known what Gracie Ann had been up to in her teenage days, the punishment she usually got would have been far more severe. That's not to say Mama never had a wild day. I know from Granny D that she did, but Gracie Ann's motive was different. Mama was a normal teenager. Gracie has always been trying to achieve a state of nirvana, but back then believed that drugs would give her an edge. All I know is I had told her to stay away from drugs and Eddie, figuring the basis of their friendship was a mutual love of debauchery and pot. Gracie Ann and Eddie have been friends since childhood, so I was used to them running around together. I had no idea that Eddie had invited her over to the garage after it was closed. Well, everyone in the school knew what that meant. Gracie Ann had come home, all dreamy-eyed, saying he had taught her something that would change her life forever. She was only fifteen. I should have been a better sister, consoled her, but my reputation was at stake too. I had never "debauched" (well, only once), and I've never smoked weed. To keep my goody-two-shoes image intact, I had slammed the door in her face. Not long after her night with Eddie on the naugahyde couch, she swore off drugs forever. The thing is, she never acted upset about what had happened, and she still brings him apple-spiced Bundt cakes for Christmas.

I can make Bundt cakes. It is actually a brand of cake pan. There's nothing hoity-toity or fancy about it. I can make these cakes, whatever flavor you want. I don't have to buy them in a shop. Gracie Ann was never good at cooking though. She can barely make a bowl of cereal. She always puts too much milk, too many flakes, and something always sloshes over the side of the bowl.

I don't know why I thought of all this as I headed for a shower and a change of clothes before helping Granny in the kitchen. I had no need to make Eddie a cake. His son James was in the living room with Lucy watching television. Her candy bracelet was spread out on the coffee table and they were eating it. I figured they were watching cartoons, so I smiled at them and went to my room.

I should have paid more attention, because when I got back to the living room, Lucy and James were locked in some Lambada-style dance on top of the coffee table. Jake the dog was their only audience. Hips together and bodies gyrating, this was not the ballet Lucy had been studying. I grabbed Lucy, legs still kicking out in dance like a bug turned upside down, and put her on the sofa. To James, I pointed "down."

"What were you doing?" I asked.

"Dancing."

My senses returning, I heard the songs before I looked to the television. They were watching *Dirty Dancing*.

"This is too old for you." I turned off the television and took out the DVD.

I looked at James. Would coffee tables be his naugahyde couch? I said to him, "Go outside and play, now!"

With a naughty smile, he left the room without saying a word.

Starry came in and I asked her, holding up the DVD, "Does your mother know she has this?"

"Yeah. She bought it."

"Well, I don't think she wants Lucy dancing like that."

"Lucy's obsessed with it. She loves Patrick Swayze."

Lucy pouted. "Aunt Faith, but I love this movie. I want to be a dancer."

"Embrace the crazy" was starting to embrace my little Lucy and make her loopy. I had to steer her back to my side.

"That's not dancing, honey. What about ballet and tap? I'm going to get you a nice video about Margot Fonteyn and you can dance like her, okay?"

Starry snorted. Lucy shrugged, pouted a little, and looked at me with her big blue eyes. "You like her?"

I nodded. "She was made a Dame and is one of the greatest ballerinas of all time."

"Okay, then." Content, she turned the television back on and flipped to cartoons. A normal child again.

When I was shelling purple hull peas in the kitchen, James

came in from being outside. My fingers were already stained purple; his were stained with tractor grease.

"Where's your daddy? I want to talk to him. You know better than to be dancing like that," I said.

"I like to mambo."

He washed his hands very carefully, cleaning each fingernail. He inspected his work when he was finished.

"Paso doble, rumba, samba. Do you watch dance sport?" he asked.

I shook my head.

"My dad takes me folk dancing. It's in a barn." His voice sounded like a child, but the way he spoke, the inflection was adult. A bushel of fresh corn was beside me on the floor. James picked up an ear, sat beside me, and starting shucking.

"This is the food of my people," he said very matter-of-fact. "Maze, they called it."

He didn't look like he had a Native American bone in his body. He did have dark eyes, but he looked more like Eddie's mother. She had the same red hair as James. He looked at me with the same probing, serious expression as his father. "I'm sorry your mom died. Do you want to talk about it?"

Caught off guard, I had to pause for a moment. "No, James, finish shucking the corn. That's very sweet of you to ask."

"You can cook with the husks," James said. "Wrap food in them and bake."

"I know. I'm a chef," I replied.

"Interesting. Very interesting. I have a severed head."

"What?"

"Want to see it?" He reached into his pocket and pulled out a Barbie doll head.

"That's very clever, James."

"Well, I must be off," he stood up, only a few ears of maze shucked, and headed back outside, leaving as his father came inside.

His last words before he closed the door behind him were, "I like Lucy. I'll do the honorable thing and marry her. I'll have a talk with her parents later." Then in a whisper, he added, "Mention nothing of what has transpired here as I want my proposal to remain a surprise."

"Where's Granny?" Eddie asked, as if oblivious to James' words.

"In the storage room."

Eddie walks slowly like he is never in a hurry. I heard him say a few words to Granny about the tractor being fixed, then he casually strolled back through the kitchen. He stopped to wash his hands too, just as carefully as James had done. I respected this trait immensely.

"Come outside and join me for a smoke," he said.

"I don't smoke."

"Join me anyway."

James and Lucy were playing on the old tire swing in the back, so we walked around to the front and sat in the porch swing. Eddie didn't say anything for awhile, just hand-rolled a cigarette and smoked. We looked like an old married couple watching the world go by.

"Did you hear what your son was doing earlier?"

"Your Granny D is not well," he said, ignoring me. Calm voice as always, still staring into the distance.

"What do you mean she's not well? I just watched her wrestle Ruthie Weston."

"She fought another old lady." He turned to me with that serious expression, eyes squinted. "I've been keeping an eye on her, but it's hard. I have a family of my own to look after."

"You've been watching out for Granny?"

"And your mom."

I looked off into the distance. I had to know. "Were you with my mother when she died?"

"I was."

"You need to talk to Gracie Ann, because she thinks ... "

"I have."

"The ribbon thing?"

He smiled. "Is it so hard to believe?"

"Yes!"

He took a long drag from his cigarette, held it, and exhaled.

"What's wrong with Granny D?" I asked.

"She's eighty-four."

"That's not a sickness."

He snuffed out his cigarette and patted me on the head like a child. "Enjoy your time here in case you don't make it back for another twenty years." He walked away. In the distance, I heard him yell, "James, time to go home."

Chapter 9

There is a rose bush underneath my bedroom window. Granny
D planted it there after one of my mother's many adventures sneaking
out of the house as a girl. Her reasoning was that Mama wouldn't be
able to climb over the thorny bush. Growing up, Mama was a lot more
like Gracie Ann, always up for an adventure, always a little flighty. In
bed by nine o'clock, homework finished, and next day's outfit laid out,
I was never like my mother in that way. She looked perfect, but she
was much more lighthearted and whimsical than me. Mama could
laugh off a cake that came out lopsided, while I can never do things like
that. My letter "I's" have the dot placed perfectly over the stem. My
bookshelf is like a library, everything arranged alphabetically. The
clothing in my closet is arranged by color, material, and season. When
I was a toddler, I would point at any open cabinet and make a grunting
noise to let someone know it needed to be shut. Everything has to be in
its place.

That's not to say our house was in disarray. I took care of that.

By looking at Mama's immaculately pressed clothes, perfectly coiffed hair, or polished shoes, you would never guess she was sometimes okay with letting dishes get crusty in the sink, or piling up throw pillows haphazardly on the sofa. I used to think it was because of her lupus. She didn't want to think about the small things. I also used to think she would die any day. The sun would come and shrivel her like a raisin, or her joints would freeze up and she'd fall to her death down a flight of stairs, or even worse, her organs would all shut down and she'd drop like a brick over breakfast. I thought if I kept everything perfect, then she would not die.

I hate to admit that I take more after Granny D when it comes to perfectionism. Her kitchen is organized like a television studio, everything is at your fingertips, everything is clean, and there is no clutter. I spent a good part of my childhood at her feet, or standing on a box so I could reach the counter top and watch her cook. As a child I probably had more flour in my hair than dirt. Gracie Ann would plod into the kitchen layered in gunk from making mud pies. It's ironic, she was quite good at that type of "cooking," the make-believe. She liked to let the "pies" harden on the porch, then decorate them with flowers and twigs.

She used the roses from the bush outside my bedroom window many times. Granny never kept the rose bush in good shape, but it usually bloomed anyway. As a teen, Gracie Ann trampled the bush a few times, trying to sneak in. I only did it once, my one night to "debauch." My friends Tiffany, Julie, and Tracey had rented a suite at the Peabody, but it was called the Excelsior Hotel then, and threw a party two days before graduation. We wanted to go out in style, but knew our parents would not let us have a hotel party. It was all done on the sly. It was my only "wild night" as a teenager, the night I got drunk and lost my virginity to Donnie Thompson. Full football scholarship to LSU, he moved away and I never saw him again. I wasn't heartbroken though. It was but one step on my road to adulthood, which I had been waiting for my whole life.

Instinctively, Granny D knew what I had done. High from sex and booze, I trampled the rose bush pretty badly. One of the thorns got me good in the leg. Granny noticed the bandage. I had shuffled off with a shrug like it was no bid deal. "You end up pregnant," she had said, frying eggs like she was discussing the weather, "and you'll be stuck here in Mulberry. That scholarship to Harvard won't mean a hill of beans." I had stood there, hand frozen to the back door like a child's tongue stuck to a metal pole on a winter day. "Do you love that boy?" she had asked, and I shook my head no. Love really meant nothing to me then, but the part about being stuck in Mulberry Field stayed with me. "Well, then, what's the point, if you don't love him?" had been her final words to me that morning. She had always talked about love as if it were a tangible object like an orange. "You gotta have the passion, burning embers and loins to make a marriage last," she had said to me before I married Stephan. "If you don't have that, it'll burn out like a swift wind blowin' through a fireplace" Just like my romp with Don nie, Granny had known my marriage to Stephan was pointless. Like Gracie Ann always says, it was Granny's sixth sense. I don't think I have a sixth sense at all. I guess I am like my dad in that way. I never see things coming. I certainly don't grasp things before they happen, can't read someone's mind, and am not good at judging situations or people without hearing it come out of their mouth. My intuition about some things is good, I suppose, but not about people, not about things in my family. If ever one was to have a sixth sense about anything, you'd think it would be about your own family.

Face-up and spread-eagle on my bed, I stared at the hole in the ceiling when I heard Uncle John and Aunt Jane arrive. There was laughter, hugs I knew took place without me seeing, and moments of quiet, a silence I knew was for Mama. To lose a sister, to lose a child, to lose a mother, did it all feel the same or different? If I lost Granny D, what would I do?

I got up and looked out the window. Dead. The rose bush was dried and cracked, rotted twigs. If I stepped on it now, it would turn to dust. Although unable to see into the future, I knew my child would never sneak out this window, never get jabbed by this rose's thorns.

There was a cheerful tap, tap, tappity tap on my door. Gracie Ann. The door opened. "Hey ya," she said.

"Hey ya, back at ya."

"There's no escape."

"Do you remember the rose bush?"

"Yes," she said, closed the door, and sat on the bed. "Did it bloom?"

"It's dead."

"It bloomed last year."

I sat beside her. "Is Granny ill?"

She got off the bed and pretended to look at things on the dresser. "Where's Beary Gordy?" He was probably still on the floor, or Jake had ran off to destroy him, thinking it a new plush for him.

"Why didn't you tell me?" I asked.

"Remember when you lost that cheerleading championship?" she said, popping an old barrette open and closed that she found on the dresser.

"Stop changing the subject."

"I'm not. Do you remember that?"

"Of course. We should have won."

"But you didn't. Everyone thought you were okay with it. You went about your day, bowed out gracefully, even though you thought you'd been wronged. Mama went into your room and you had destroyed all your cheerleading things, just busted it up, and you were balling your eyes out."

"What's your point?"

"Or when Poppy hurt his hand on the tractor and everyone thought he would be damaged for life ... "

"But he wasn't."

"But you freaked out, Faith. Completely freaked out." She found Beary Gordy on the floor and put him back in his usual spot.

"That's just my point. You freak out over stuff. You appear calm and collected to the world, but you can't handle any stress. Not even a little."

"I can."

"Can't. Everything has to be perfect for you. Absolutely. Positively. Perfect."

"So."

"So. I didn't want you to freak out. With Mama getting worse, I just ... "

I got up. "I had to hear this stuff about Granny D from Eddie. You couldn't even tell me."

"She's not dying, Faith. She just can't get around as well anymore."

"She seems fine to me."

"You haven't been home in twenty years. You can't judge a person by phone calls ... "

"Let's not start with that."

She put up her hands in defeat over a fight that did not happen. "She's slowing down. I asked Eddie to keep an eye on her when he can, not let her take on too much. You know how she is. She's worse than you. She could have a stake rammed into her head and act like nothing was wrong."

"You should have told me. We could get a nurse for her. You didn't have to ask Eddie."

She laughed. "Yeah right. Granny D would scare the shit out of a nurse. Besides, I trust Eddie more than some hired nurse."

"I wouldn't." I looked her over. "I can't believe you two are still so ... chummy after all these years."

She gave me a funny look. "Chummy? What's that suppose to mean?"

"Oh, please. Apple-spiced Bundt cake," I replied with malice in my voice – the voice of someone who thinks they have trapped a criminal in a lie. But it was me who got caught.

She pondered it like it were absurd. "We've been friends for years. What's the big deal?" Like a row of criminals in a line-up, she fingered me, found out the truth with one slip-up on my part. Gracie Ann laughed wickedly, as if told the funniest of jokes, even putting her hand on her stomach. "You like Eddie." She pointed at me, accusing. I half expected a chorus of "K-I-S-S-I-N-G."

"Give me a break. I don't like that greasy-haired mechanic."

"He's not a greasy-haired mechanic."

Suddenly I was Karo syrup. I mustered the sweetest "syrupiest" voice I could think of. "Oh, Eddie, spin me around like a little school girl ... ooh!"

"You really like him. You're so jealous." She said this through more laughter. My sticky sweetness did not stick to her.

"I'm not jealous."

"You are. Don't be jealous of me because I have friends, Faith."

"I have friends."

"No, you have socialites."

"And I guess you have Eddie Field." I started to leave and yanked open the bedroom door.

"Run away, Faith, like always. You see what you're doing? You're avoiding this conversation, too. Too much stress. Not part of your perfect world. Eddie, I mean, it's ridiculous, right?"

I whispered to her so no one in the other room could hear. "You're out of your gourd, Gracie. You're the one who should be avoiding it. Heaven forbid, Jonesy were to find out ... "

"Find out what?"

"It's obvious." Smirk.

She slapped me. Never in our sisterhood have we ever laid hands upon one another. Any unresolved anger came out now like a can of soda that had been shaken by a machine that stirs paint. We ripped into one another and things got messy. She grabbed me by the hair and slung me onto the bed. Like children, we wrestled, falling to the floor. I kicked her in the stomach; she heaved, then jabbed her knee into my lower back.

That's how Uncle John found us, one sister who looked like she was about to hurl, the other one with a mess of formerly perfectly-combed hair. If Eddie had seen us, he would have said the same thing he had said earlier, "You Dunleys are always up for a good fight," because again my shirt was torn and I looked crazed.

Technically, we are only half Dunley, and I try to stress that fact. It's hard to get that point across when you get caught holding your sister down by the ankles. Even though Gracie Ann has never fought the crazy, she embraces her Orion blood too. She has a tattoo of the constellation Orion on her ankle. At first it looked like a bunch of un-connected black dots, but she recently had lines drawn in, and now it resembles the Greek hunter shooting arrows off her ankle.

Granny D shot off a few jabs of her own. Like teenagers in trouble, we sat in the kitchen with Granny shaking her head at us. "This is not how sisters are suppose to behave," she said to us. Our faces had the same pout that Starry had when she got caught with the Weston boy. "On the eve of your mother's funeral! Family shouldn't fight like that. You want me to find a bow and arrow so you can shoot at one another? Would that be all right? Huh? Huh? Behaving like that!"

Ashamed, I helped Granny finish making lunch for everyone. I got the better end of the deal, because Gracie Ann had to "entertain" the family which is not an "entertaining" thing to do. I heard Uncle John quote a *Bible* verse. Meekly, Aunt Jane affirmed his statements with an occasional "amen." After our fight, Aunt Jane had merely filed the information away like some executive document in a file cabinet like she did at Wal-Mart headquarters. We were suddenly juice on-sale or a new employee dress code, nothing to worry about, but let everyone know and keep it on hand for future reference.

"What were you two fightin' about anyway?" Granny D asked, tossing a salad.

We certainly couldn't tell anyone what had caused the argument. "Just upset about everything, I guess," I said back and looked at her carefully. She appeared to be the picture of perfect health for anyone her age. Spry, got around well, mental faculties appeared normal for the most part. "Granny, do you feel all right?"

"I'm fine, sweetie, although my ass is sore after fallin' down Ruthie's steps. Damn those Westons!"

"No, I mean, in general, are you okay?"

She gave me a sour look. "I don't want to hear this. I'm fine. Now go get everyone. Tell 'em lunch is on." I got up and she added, "Don't you start like Gracie and Eddie. They're cluttering up your mind with nonsense. I can use an extra hand now and then, but so could anyone. I'm running an entire house by myself, tending a field ... "

"Granny, you can let the garden go. Why do you need all that? Just plant a small one out back."

"A small one? A small one?" Granny never kept her anger bottled up like a shaken soda can. She popped it open. "Since I moved to this property, your Poppy and I have planted purple hull peas, tomatoes, and corn. Sometimes watermelons. I don't intend to stop." She looked up into the air. "You hear that, Pops? Plant a small one."

"I just thought maybe you could let Eddie do it for you."

"He can help." She yelled to the front room, "Lunch!" Before they came in, she asked me, "Where'd he go anyway?"

"Who, Granny? Poppy?" I thought for a moment she might be a little senile. After all, she did still talk to him.

"No. What do you think, I'm crazy? Eddie. Where's he at? He was out back fixing my tractor."

"He left after he finished. Remember he came in and told you?"

"Must have slipped my mind," she said and ushered everyone to the table. "Faith, after lunch, you plan on finishin' shellin' those purple hull peas?"

I nodded; everyone took a seat, quietly. Purple hull peas were my mother's favorite. Black-eyed peas were fine, but it was the purple hull ones that she really liked. We were making those in her honor, along with fried chicken, mashed potatoes, fried corn, and wilted lettuce. I planned to make a chocolate cake and an apple pie, using the apples from Ol' man Wilson's orchard. Gracie Ann was in charge of snacks. One thing she can cook is Chex Mix. She can also put things on crackers. I think it comes from living in Los Angeles. She can make finger foods for parties. Jonesy likes to entertain, have parties, invite studio executive and "celebrities" over for dinner. Usually Gracie Ann has the affairs catered, but she likes to make little hors d'oeuvre, the simple ones you would see on any coffee table.

I didn't think any of her girls, even Lucy, had inherited the love of cooking, so I was shocked when Night came to me after lunch and asked if she could make something for Mama's funeral. She wanted to make strawberry shortcake.

"You don't want to use those store-bought packaged cakes. We can make fresh," I told her.

"But I don't know how."

"I can show you. It's not hard."

Starry came in and got involved too. Granny D looked at her, pointed at the fresh strawberries, and said, "You see, fresh strawberries. Always use fresh. That's the key to great cooking." Lucy propped up a chair and watched intently. Before long, it was like I had my own cooking class. Making food hadn't made me laugh or smile in a long while. It was merely my job. I helped Night stir the batter, observed Starry cutting strawberries, and tasted the whipped cream that Lucy had just mixed. Everything was perfect.

Somewhere along the way I had shirked off my responsibilities to the purple hull peas, so I picked up a pile and started shelling, as I watched the girls make the shortcake. Gracie Ann, escaping the continuing front room *Bible* lesson, looked at us all there. "Oh, great, don't you make my girls all anal and shi-shi like you." It was suppose to be an insult, but it was said with a smile.

Chapter 10

My sister met Jonesy at USC. She was working toward her art degree; he was working on his master's thesis film project. He saw her reading a book about 1950s sci-fi movies and approached her. He loved her look – blond, pretty, and nutty – and cast her in his film. After she graduated, they were married right before I moved to New York with Stephan. I'll never forget that first meeting. Jonesy had grabbed my hand, shook it firmly, and smiled this wild smile the whole time. It was as if the entire world fascinated him like a baby discovering a bug walking across the porch. "Would you look at that?" he said about everything. Jonesy's a tornado, gathering up speed, and taking in everything in his path along the way. Sometimes he leaves everything in shambles, other times it is a fun ride, leaving you somewhere you've never been before.

As Jonesy recounted his tale of having met an A-list actor with his usual extroverted vigor, I was stuck conversing with cousin Tootie

and the person she was rooming with in Scott, who looked like a
jezebel from a turn-of-the-century burlesque show, feather boa and all.
Uncle John kept giving this girl the eye and not in a good way. I knew
he was itching to preach the word to her. Uncle Henry kept giving her
the eye too, but in a completely different way all together. He wanted
to complement her on the boa.

"So, I said to him, 'Mr. Depp, thank you for the compliment.
It means, wow, the world.' He shook my hand and finished his bacon
sandwich," Jonesy said, taking a puff from his pipe, proud as a stage
mother whose daughter just won a beauty pageant. "He knew *my*
films." He puffed up his chest, goofy wild smile.

I leaned over Tootie and her friend, whispered to Gracie Ann,
"Did this happen?"

She nodded. "But I really doubt he knew any of Glen's films.
Why spoil it for him though? I let him have his moment."

Jonesy continued, "It's not the A-listers that really touch me
though. It's the real people, when they come up and say hello, or write
a nice letter. Not too long ago, these two delightful teenagers, went by
the names of Travis Edwards and Aubrey Clover, wrote to tell me how
much they loved my movies. So sweet. Well, I wrote them back immediately and sent some autographed DVDs priority mail."

"I met David Duchovny once. Charming man. Absolutely
lovely," Uncle Henry replied, his voice a tad higher than the last time
I'd seen him. Hormones, Gracie Ann had told me earlier. Luckily, he
hadn't shown up in drag, but he sounded like Marilyn Monroe with a
chest cold.

"You don't say, Henry," Jonesy replied. Genuine interest.
"Did you happen to get any contact info? I'm making a new sci-fi picture soon."

As they talked Hollywood bullshit, I bowed out as gracefully
as possible. Outside, I looked up to the sky, saw a full moon and observed the constellation Orion, imagined that my parents were in the
sky together like Osiris and Isis. Nothing as heroic or interesting as an

Egyptian myth, but my parent's marriage started out peculiar like everything else in my family. One of them had the key to a new car. A radio station had given out keys to lucky callers throughout the summer of 1968. The station's morning DJ was nicknamed "Green Bean," and the car they were giving away promoted his show. It was a pea-colored '68 four-door Nova with the vanity plate "Bean" and a pair of fuzzy beans that hung from the rearview mirror like a set of giant lizard testicles. The car was officially nicknamed "The Bean." My parents each had a key; neither had ever met. They stood next to each other, each stealing polite, interested glances at one another. About twenty or so people took their turn at the ignition. Being a bit of a butterfinger, Mama dropped her key, and Dad reached down to pick it up, dropping his in the process. She had asked, flirty, "Are you sure this one is mine? What if they got switched?" Attempting to be charming, but dead serious too, he had replied, "If either of us wins, then we have to share." Mama's response was, "Share a car? That might be difficult." The last thing Dad said before getting into "The Bean" was, "Then I guess we'll have to get married." Vroom. His key worked and six months later they got married. For their honeymoon, they took the car on a road trip to see the badlands in South Dakota. In 1970, I was born. The car stayed with us longer than Dad.

"Do you remember 'The Bean'?" I asked Gracie Ann as she came out on the porch to join me.

"That car was so ugly," she said looking up at the sky with me. "Mama almost drove it off the road that one time during the ice storm, picking us up early after school. What were you, about eight? I was in kindergarten, I think."

"Everyone made fun of it. I preferred riding the bus."

"It was so embarrassing," she said.

"The Bean." Lost in memory.

"Our Mama was a dork, you know."

"Indeed. But she was our dork."

Gracie Ann smiled. "Indeed. Only you say 'indeed.' You're a dork, too."

"Indeed ... I am not."

"Let's go up to the house before I have to put the girls to bed. Granny can finish up in the kitchen now. It's either that or listen to more of Glen's stories."

"No more stories!" I said, hands up.

We walked up the driveway. Gravel rocks, stickers, weeds, and a few loose puffs of unharvested cotton were at my feet as I walked along the road. Gracie Ann picked up a rock and hurled it down the road.

"I can hit that tree," she said, picking up another stone. I nodded, tempting her to try. She reared her arm way back and threw it. Ding! It hit the pine tree in the distance with a solid thud. A piece of bark chipped off.

"Whatever happened to that tree house?" I asked.

"Don't you remember? Same ice storm, too much weight, and it collapsed."

"Oh yeah."

"We thought we could live there, remember? Our vast empire."

I smiled. Poppy had built it for us, and we played "house" in it every chance we could. It was my trial run for adulthood.

"What's going to become of this place when Granny D dies?" Gracie Ann asked.

I stopped walking. "Don't say that."

"She will. I mean, you know, eventually. What then, Faith? I don't ever want to sell it."

I could see the house now. The porch light was on. No lights inside. It was like we were coming home after watching late night television with Granny and Poppy. Mama already in bed, left the front porch light on for us to see.

"What about you and Jonesy? You could move back with the kids. Keep an eye on Granny."

She shook her head. "That's not possible. I don't want to

move back anymore than you." She looked up at the sky again. "It's our past. How do you put that away? I can't imagine someone else walking this road, sleeping in our old rooms, picking our mulberries. Some stranger."

"Me either," I said.

"But it'll rot if we don't take care of it, if no one lives in either house."

"Let's just cross that bridge when we come to it, okay?" I said, not wanting to think about it anymore.

We opened our front door, flicked on the lights inside, and as if by magic, the house seemed alive again. It looked lived-in with opened suitcases, dirty dishes on the coffee table, the scent of fresh showers lingering from the bathroom. Gracie Ann stood by the fireplace, rested her arm on the ledge, and said, "Want some wine?" She went to the kitchen and came back with two glasses and a bottle of wine. Together on the sofa, we sipped it without talking, both wishing we had some wood to burn in the fireplace even though the temperature outside was warm.

"I have an idea. You're not going to like it," she said finally, breaking the tranquil feel of the night. "I asked a book what we should do."

"Huh?"

"The idea is that there are no real coincidences, right? So, you pick any book, ask a question about whatever – who's my soulmate, what should I do about this or that – then open the book at random and point. Whatever you land on is the answer."

I nearly choked on my wine. "That's the stupidest thing I've ever heard. You aren't serious?"

"I've gotten some eerie answers."

"Gracie Ann ... "

"I thought maybe Eddie and his family could move in here."

"Are you nuts?"

"It'll be easier for him to keep an eye on Granny."

"First of all, we can't ask him to watch our grandmother." Biting my lip, I added, "He has his own family."

"They'll be better off here. I've told him that."

"It doesn't look right."

She took a long drink, looked at me, and said, "You really think we have something going on, don't you?"

"Do you?"

"No." She took another drink, laughed a little, the wine starting to take effect. "You're jealous." She poked at me playfully.

"Stop it. I'm not jealous." I finished off my glass. "You have to realize how it looks. What does Jonesy, Glen, think?"

"He loves Eddie. Glen knows the truth, unlike *some* people."

"I'm just saying ... "

"I don't give a fuck what other people think, Faith. He's my friend. I'm trying to help him out. Have you seen that yurt he lives in?"

"Yogurt?"

She snorted with laughter. The wine was getting to both of us. "No! Yurt. He lives in a yurt."

"What's a yurt?"

She stood up, made a big circle with her hands. She looked like she was imitating a pregnant woman. "It's this big round teepee-like thing, I swear."

"Goodness."

She sat back down. "He built it himself. It's very small. He lives there with ..." She burped, laughed, and went on, "His granddad and son."

"You want to give him free rent?"

"He'll pay rent." She scooted onto the floor, kicked her legs out in front of her. "Just admit you like him."

I scooted down next to her. "I don't."

"Admit it or I'm calling him and telling him myself."

"Grow up."

"I'll do it." She crawled over to the phone.

I took another drink, pretended not to be afraid of her dare. She started to dial. "He's married anyway," I said.

She put the phone down. "He's not married."

"He wears a wedding ring. Who's James' mother then?"

"Mindy."

"Mindy? Not Janet?"

"Janet? Who? No, you're confused."

I was indeed. "Explain."

"His high school sweetheart. Mindy. Remember? They dated all through school."

"I never knew he dated anyone," I said, then giving her a smirk, added, "Slept with plenty."

She ignored my comment. "Mindy Duncan. She went to Mills High in Little Rock. Real sweet, shy girl. You never met her?"

I shook my head and racked my brain trying to remember. The most vivid image I ever had of him in high school was seeing him play guitar on the steps before class. He always looked like a hoodlum. Girls used to crowd around and listen to him play, but everyone knew he wasn't the "let's go steady" type.

"They got married after they both finished college and ... "

"He went to college?" I said surprised.

She nodded. "You see, there you go again. Just like everyone else in school, you put a lot of bull on him, making judgements without knowing him." Gracie Ann got real serious. "He had a B-average in school. Did you know that? Everyone thought he was a dope head, a loser, a hoodlum. He wasn't."

"I didn't know him very well. Wasn't part of my clique."

"You were a snob. You're still a snob." She lightly nudged me and giggled.

I shrugged. "What happened with him and Mindy? Why'd they divorce?"

"They didn't divorce. She died in childbirth around the same time you got your show. You didn't know all of this? Shit, I know I told you."

I shrugged again.

"I remember it was really hard for him struggling with the joy of having a child and the pain of losing the woman he loved," she said.

Something about the word "love" made me uneasy. It didn't have the soured beans taste of the word "dead," but it made me queasy just the same when I thought about Eddie and Mindy.

"He won't take that wedding ring off. It's stuck like ... what's a good metaphor?"

"Geez, Gracie, I don't know."

"His own mother died in childbirth, too," she said.

"I knew that." I drank more wine.

"Weird."

"So who's Janet?"

"What? I don't know."

"Granny brought her up."

"Hmmm." She poured two more glasses of wine. "Maybe that's the girl he's been seeing?" Gracie Ann looked at me closely. "Real pretty one. She models for this clothing line."

"Oh."

"Ah-ha! You grimaced! You *do* like him!"

"Please."

"Yes, you do. I saw the hint of jealousy."

"No."

"Just admit it."

"What difference does it make? We aren't compatible."

"Are you sure?"

"Yes."

"I lied. There is no girlfriend. I don't know anything about this Janet person."

"Who was he up at Mulberry Pointe with then?"

"When was he up there?" Gracie Ann asked.

I could not tell her about Eddie catching Starry up there with the Weston boy. "I just happened to see him."

"Oh, well, I guess he is seeing someone then. I'll have to ask him about that. I'll report back to you."

"No reporting back. Just let it go, Gracie."

We sat there for a long while, lost in our thoughts, getting drunk, not thinking about tomorrow.

Chapter 11

In my grandparent's front yard there used to be a big oak tree. It lumbered, loomed, and protected the front porch for years. Gracie Ann liked to climb it. A tornado destroyed it. I remember all of us – Mama, Granny & Poppy, Gracie Ann & I – huddling in the storage room. We had all been at my grandparents when the storm had started. Poppy D said we should head down to our house. Brick is stronger than wood. It came on too fast though, swept by before we could bundle up and make a mad dash home. They say tornados sound like an oncoming train, but you expect a train to roll down the tracks. You see the tracks, the headlight coming toward you. You wait its arrival. You never expect, no matter how many news reports warn you, for a tornado to set tail in your yard. When it happens it is not like an approaching train. Trains stay on course. The only way it can hurt you is for you to stand on the tracks, deliberately getting in its path. Tornados are alive and chaotic. They jump and skip like children playing hopscotch. Where they land is a mere lucky or unlucky roll of the dice. Poppy was right about brick being stronger than wood. The tornado dared not touch our house. It may have tried like the Big Bad Wolf, but to no avail. Like a snarly, angry boxer's side jab, it touched Granny & Poppy's house indirectly, flicking that big oak tree off its roots and into the air like a man tossing his hat onto a rack. It crashed into the front porch, caving it like a piece of crumpled tin foil. It sounded like war. Not that I knew what war sounded like, but that's what I had imagined. In my mind, it was the H-bomb landing. I had thought we were all going to die. I was about to turn fourteen that summer. It was spring. Poppy had just planted the field. Mama had a bad rash brought on by hay fever and her lupus. Her face was red and she was crying, holding onto her girls for life. She had hovered over us as if her body could protect us. I thought, looking at her back then, that she looked like a person who had been burned. If she died, they would find this woman and not realize how beautiful she is, was. I had put my hands on her hair, tried to straighten it, but she had quickly pushed them away, put me underneath her like a mother duck protecting her chicks. That's when we heard it. BOOM! CRASH! That glorious magnificent tallest of tall trees with its heavy limbs for climbing protecting sheltering went down. Gone. Just like that. The next day Gracie Ann and I climbed on it. We had fun surveying the tippy top of the tree no one was ever brave enough to climb all the way to its peak. It was lifeless. Leaves already turning brown, even though they had just turned green only weeks before. I had picked up a leaf, looked at its brown, reddish hue and thought the same thing I had thought of Mama. It looked like it had been in a fire. Brittle, it crumbled in my hand. How could something that was so strong only hours before be so wilted now? Could anything really have that much force? I went to the big hole in the ground, its former nesting place, a few roots jutted out, as if looking for their former love lost in a great battle. Was there anything left? Anyone hiding in the rubble that we loved? Any hope? I had cried as I sat alone in the hole. Gracie Ann had come over and pounced me like a cat.

  "Stop crying," she had said. "It's just a tree. A new one will grow."

  But it never did. From that point on, the landscape was different. Home was different.

It's ironic that was also the year that brought the best crop we ever had. It was like Osiris himself had ordained the land to be fertile, flooded, and prosperous. Wildflowers were everywhere and the trees, those that survived the wrath, looked greener. Ordained to live. Ordained to be born again.

Ready to go to the funeral, I was on the front porch when Granny D came outside. Yellow and black. Put us together and we looked like a bumble bee. While I went with a traditional black dress for the funeral, Granny D picked a yellow sundress and hat. The outfit was the same one she wore on my fourteenth birthday. That day is still one of my favorite days of my entire life. In the summer of 1984, I had a huge birthday party, got my driver's permit, and let Sullivan McGee feel my bourgeoning boobs. I had since long forgotten that fallen tree in a matter of months. We had finally installed cable television and blasted MTV most of the day. Mama put on a magic show, mostly card tricks she learned from a late night program, with Gracie Ann and Eddie as her "magician's assistants." My presents, I remember well, were a pair of white roller skates, the *Purple Rain* soundtrack (on LP), and a pink faux diamond ring. I can't really say why this particular day is one of my favorites other than everyone was in a good mood. It was one of those days when the entire family was together, the summer heat seemed unimportant, and I was starting to feel like an adult. That day, that leap into adulthood, I knew was very close. Becoming an adult is like crossing from one state line to the next. You see the sign, but the scenery doesn't change immediately. There's no difference between Texarkana, Arkansas and Texarkana, Texas. Drive west, and the farther you drive into Texas, you start to see subtle differences. Before long, you're all the way into the deserts of New Mexico, and you realize just how far you've gone.

As an adult, I looked out at the worst day ahead of me. Just like my teenage birthday, the front porch was lined with a variety of flowers, but there were no balloons, no gifts, no laughing faces gorging on chocolate cake. And there was still no big protective oak tree.

Eddie honked his horn as he drove by and saw us on the porch. Granny waved him back; he backed up his truck in the middle of the road and pulled into the front of the house. I had never seen him in a suit before. I don't even recall him wearing one at our graduation. All in black attire, shiny loafers, and pressed green handkerchief in his jacket pocket to match his green tie, he looked like a man about to make an entrance at a fancy party. He hugged Granny and I, then she asked, "Can you make drop biscuits?"

"I can, I guess," he said, a little surprised, which surprised me. His face is always one of confidence.

"Come by the house before the grave site services and make them. I want them to be fresh. We should have biscuits," she said, looked around, like a person trying to remember something but she really had nothing to remember, other than memories. "They never come out right for me."

He kissed her on the cheek and nodded. "I'll get everything ready. Don't worry."

"Thank you," I said to him.

Granny gave him a rundown of the things that needed to be put out; she and I would handle the rest when we arrived.

"You wouldn't happen to have any Band-Aids?" he asked. "James cut his finger this morning playing with one of Papa's rocks. Had a sharp bit on it. I was on my way to get some."

That little boy cut his hand, I thought to myself, and Eddie wanted to heal it. Something sweet was welling up in me like yeast rising a cake.

Granny D went inside and left Eddie and I alone on the front porch.

"You doin' all right?" he asked me.

"I'll be fine."

Amid the funerary flowers, near the front door on a ratty discarded end-table was a bouquet of tulips from Stephan's mother. Continuing his book tour, Wee Ste-fan was in the French Riviera with the woman he left me for, a French model with no breasts, no brains, and no beauty. Stephan's mother, Mrs. Moreau, like my mother, has an old-fashioned look. She's Clara Bow with a soft-spoken voice and short, curly hair, but our mothers did not get along. After our wedding, a small affair in Corsica, they rarely spoke. I had wanted them to be friends, imagined them hanging out like a female buddy movie come to life in vivid color. They would gossip on the phone, shop for fancy dresses, drink wine. But none of that ever happened. They dealt with each other because they had to, like dealing with the phone company when the line goes dead. Wee Ste-fan's father never had the chance to pal around with my father, of course. I had fantasized about that, too. Dad, young Kris Kringle look that he had, walking the vineyards with Mr. Moreau, who you knew played polo and ate wild pheasant just by looking at him. He is European to the core; his heartbeat probably drums out the French national anthem, *La Marseillaise*. Always ready with a goofy joke, Mama had said my father was all-American, could recite The Preamble, played football in college, and built things with his bare hands. Wee Ste-fan's father polished his nails.

It is amazing who gets along though. I never really knew Eddie, but he has been in my life for as far back as I can remember. He was like a potted plant that I never tended, yet it survived. His hair flicked in the breeze, jutted up on his head for a moment, partially covering my line of sight into the front yard where the oak used to stand. Standing on the front porch, sniffing the tulips from Stephan's mother, it seemed like Eddie belonged there more than store-bought floral arrangements and well-wishes on greeting cards.

Eddie looked back up at me with piercing eyes. I looked away. He pulled me against him, rested his chin on my head, but he couldn't shelter me from the feelings that finally rolled down the tracks like an approaching train. I buried my face in his neck and cried. I heard the front door open then close quietly. Granny D did not come outside.

"I can't go, Eddie. Don't make me."

"You have to. You'll regret it for the rest of your life."

"No. Please. I can't see her in that casket. I just can't."

I did not go to my mother's funeral. It passed by me like the wind, like I was brick. I shook it off like a bad nightmare, cleaned up the pieces like we did after the tornado, believing in a few months time, I would forget all about it.

Chapter 12

I prefer winter. You can get warm. A blanket can be carried.
You can bundle, layer yourself in clothes. But heat resides all around
you like a fog, sticks to you like goo, melting you like magma from a
volcano. Cool can't be carried around artificially. An air conditioner
only radiates a certain radius of cool. Step out of it and you are hot
again. Iced tea, paper plate folded in half to make a fan, or even ice
cream, none of them really cool you down. The heat outside the day of
Mama's funeral was tremendous. I started bringing the food back inside. I thought no one would want to sit out near the picnic table. Not
today. Today was unbearable.

My other grandparents like summers. Dad's parents are so
typical you'd think they were invented for a television sitcom. They let
me take care of them, do the usual "old people" things like play bridge
and eat at buffets, and they dress appropriately for a funeral. Like I
said, they don't exactly "embrace the crazy" but it is there. The Orions

are like a big stew that has settled in the pot. You have to stir it up to get the "crazy" to come to the surface. Just stick a big spoon in there, swirl it around a few times, and you'll be surprised what rises to the surface. For instance, they live in a retirement community in Cape Canaveral, Florida, so they can see the rocket launches from the NASA base. Sounds fairly normal, right? No. See, Grandpa Orion went through the astronaut program. Now he claims he's "magnetized." He never made it to space. Grandma Orion is as thoroughly obsessed in the space odyssey, but she has been engaged in an ongoing battle with the U.S. patent office for years. She claims she invented the rear window defogger and will defend this to anyone who will listen. She's still waiting on her royalty check. Aside from all this, for the most part they are normal. Just don't mention their transvestite son.

I hadn't expected them to be in town at all. When I had called them from Boston, Grandpa's arthritis was so bad that he didn't think he could stand the plane ride. Being magnetized causes a multitude of health problems. But, there they were, hugging me with bittersweet smiles.

"Grandma, Grandpa, why didn't you tell me you were coming?" I said to them, politely wiping away the wet, old people kisses on my cheek. "When did you get in?"

"Damned airports," Grandpa Orion said. "They made me go through the metal detector. I tried to tell 'em."

Magnetized.

"I can't go through no metal detector."

Grandma Orion, used to such complaining, only shook her head and said, her voice elegant like mine, "I bought a lemon icebox pie at Safeway on the way over. I need to get it in the refrigerator."

"My fridge busted," Granny D told them and recounted the tale, as if it were a disaster film, of how she had to buy a new refrigerator.

"You did buy Sears, no doubt?" Grandpa Orion said as they went inside. I heard Gracie Ann exclaim with glee as she saw that

Grandpa and Grandma Orion were there.

Eddie's truck pulled up, being driven by Edward Sr. I saw James beside him in the front seat. Lucy, who had been toiling away sadly on the tire swing, perked up when she saw James and ran to the truck.

I walked over too and said to James, as he got out of the truck, "You look very handsome." He was cute in his suit. A little Band-Aid on his hand.

Eddie brought out the drop biscuits; they had turned out perfectly. When Granny D had returned home from the funeral, the first thing she did was take a biscuit. She looked it over, held it in her hand to judge the weight and texture of it, then she took a bite and smiled.

James and Lucy tried to grab a biscuit, but Eddie held the plate up high. "Did you wash your hands yet?" He scooted the kids off to wash up.

"Faith, why are you bringing everything indoors?" he asked me, putting the biscuits on the picnic table.

Edward Sr. replied for me. "Hot as blazes out here."

"I think Granny D wants the food outdoors," Eddie said. "Better stop carting it back inside."

Granny D and the Grandparents Orion came back outside with Gracie Ann and Jonesy, hooked arm and arm. "Eddie, have you ever met my other grandparents?" Gracie Ann asked. They had all changed into lighter attire since the weather was so warm. Earlier, all in black, the Jones family looked like they had stepped out of a gothic horror movie, especially Jonesy, who looked like Gomez Addams instead of Walt Disney. The twins looked like blond-haired versions of Wednesday Addams; they peeked out the door, having the good sense to stay near the air conditioning.

"I don't believe we have met," Eddie said, shaking hands.

Grandpa Orion hiked up his pants, as if they could get any higher, and said in a manly voice, "I heard you installed that bad boy Kenmore in there. Nice, very nice appliance. I can't install anything with a central cooling unit. Antifreeze does terrible things to my magnetism."

Before Eddie could respond with a "Huh?", I interrupted, "Grandpa, did you meet his son James?" I waved James and Lucy over as they came bounding down the steps.

"How do you do?" James said to the Orions in his adult-sounding voice and adult attire.

Charmed instantly, they were.

"I'm James Field. My father, Eddie here, is friends with your granddaughter, Gracie Ann."

"Oh. I see," said Grandma Orion. "Do you play with my little great-grandchild Lucy?"

"Lucy is my betrothed."

"There will be a wedding," Edward Sr. said. At some point, and no one knows when, he had crawled into the back of the truck. He sat up like a zombie.

Grandpa Orion nodded, played along without a flinch. "You seem like a very nice young man, James. Congratulations are in order then."

Lucy held up her hand. Upon it was a ring, the type you get for a quarter from a gum machine. Solid plastic, pebble sized "stone." Apparently, he had proposed at the funeral and Lucy had said yes.

"I'm so glad you came," Gracie Ann said again to our grandparents. "Is your arthritis, okay? You want to sit down?"

"I'll be fine," Grandpa Orion said.

Digging around in his pocket, Edward Sr. said to him, "I know just the thing." Naturally, he handed Grandpa Orion a shiny rock.

Grandpa held up his hands in fear and asked, "What's the core element in that?"

"Magnetite."

Grandpa Orion stepped back slowly.

Ignoring them, Grandma Orion looked at me and said, "Faithy dear, you look so flushed. Why don't you go lie down before everyone else gets here?"

"You do look a little warm," Eddie said.

"I've got the food all laid out," Granny D said, then turned to Eddie. "Those biscuits were perfect, boy."

"Thank you, Ma'am."

Looking at me, Granny D said, "You see what he can do."

I think Eddie actually blushed. If I looked flushed before, I certainly looked more so after Granny said that. Eddie grabbed Lucy and James by the hand and said, "Let's get some food in those bellies."

I didn't want any food in my belly, just cool air in my face. I took their advice, standing over the hot stove had made me tired, and I went to take a quick nap in my old room.

I'm the type of person who usually doesn't remember dreams. I don't have nightmares or "good dreams." I dream like anyone else, but they rarely stay with me, never seem to hold any significance. Gracie Ann can analyze a dream into the ground. She makes Sigmund Freud appear amateur.

The dream I had during my nap shook me awake like a boulder crashing into the window. In the dream Eddie held my hand as we went through double doors. If it weren't for our black clothes and somber expressions, we looked like a couple about to be married, a little unsure, a little doubt, but there was no turning back. When I stepped through the double doors, I knew this was no wedding. Before me, at the front of a zillion rows of chairs separated like the great sea, was a coffin. Like looking through a fisheye lens, it was centered in my view but seemed miles away. I could see her hands clasped on her chest, her wedding ring glinting in the sunlight that streamed in with Eddie and I. My steps were sluggish like walking through a muddy, plowed field. Each step seemed to suck me back into the earth. It felt like my knees were mired in dirt; I was slowly sinking, but I was aware I kept progressing a little closer each time. From the corner of my eye, I saw Gracie Ann's lip quiver; she bit her lip the way she always did when she held back tears. Somewhere, and it seemed miles away like Mama's coffin, was a little yelp of pain. At first I thought it was Lucy, the cry was so pure. Then I saw a yellow flash cover Mama's hand, cover the black coffin. They say everyone mourns in their own way. I thought Granny D stored her pain in jars, mixed her tears with pectin, and stashed everything in the freezer to save for a later day. Today was that day. Unleashed, opened, everything oozed out of her. It wasn't just Mama, but Poppy too, as she clutched her necklace and held Mama's hand. No one stopped her. No one rushed up to comfort her or pull her away like some melodramatic movie. Gracie Ann looked at me. As thin as a petal, as fragile as glass, her lip was bleeding from having bitten it. I was like a person who had melted in that very spot and could not move. I had never seen my mother cry, not even at Dad's funeral, and hearing Granny D wail was like seeing a child beaten, witnessing an execution, or being unable to stop a dog from being hit by a car. Helpless. Vulnerable. Pointless. None of those words had ever described Granny D, but they described me.

"Eddie, I can't," I whispered. "Take me home." He did not. We took a seat in the back. "I can't hear this," I pleaded with him. Granny D's sobbing went on for what seemed hours. "Please," I kept begging him. "Make it stop."

I saw Mama's face then. It looked like she had been crying, but it was Granny D's tears on her face. My tears were an angry mob about to break through a barricade, but the fort was strong. I did not cry. I just stared at Mama's face. I wanted to notice every detail, every wrinkle, every eyelash on her face. Imprint it in my mind forever.

The doors opened again and my mother's casket was carried out. I laughed and everyone gave me a funny look, wondering what was amusing at this time. I saw a mound of dirt. There was a flagpole atop it like on Mulberry Pointe, but next to it was a giant hole in the ground. Roots jutted out of it like the spot where the old oak tree used to stand. They put Mama's casket in the hole, vertically, letting it stand at attention. It fell open and Mama landed at my feet.

"Take me home, Eddie," I said, but Mama opened her eyes – so black they must have been dipped in the night sky like a truffle in dark chocolate. She said, "I'm not dead, Faith. Don't bury me." Like zombies, Poppy D and Dad were there, walking in a hazy slow motion, covered in dirt. They said together, "Why'd you bury us, Faith? We're still alive. We can't breathe under all that soil."

Eddie looked at me with anger, threw a set of keys at me, and said, "You buried your family alive." I reached out to embrace all of them–

Everyone has heard the expression about sitting "bolt upright" in bed after a bad dream. No one really does that, but I did with arms outstretched, holding no one. Sweat poured off me.

"Damned air conditioning," I heard Granny D yelling from outside. "Damn it! Damn it! Damn it!" There was a loud clang and then a loud wail, the same one I had heard in my dream. "Everything's fallin' apart," she screamed. I looked out the window, opened it, and could see Granny D beating the crap out of the central air unit. Everyone was outside. I looked around. It was an ocean of familiar faces. All my family, Eddie and his family, old friends from school, Ol' man Wilson, Maude, Bob from the train station. They were all there, watching Granny destroy the air conditioner. I leaned out farther, a thorn from the old rose bush pricked me. I knew I was awake even if the scene was so bizarre. The artificial air that had cooled the house was gone. The bloody heat had taken its toll. There was no way to escape it. Granny D wasn't beating the busted appliance though, not really. She was a jar of mulberry jam splattered on the floor. All her juices, all her sweet goodness, oozed everywhere. Then she stopped just as suddenly, noticed a yellow dandelion that had been hidden behind the air conditioner.

It was Jonesy who put his hand on my Granny D's back and plucked the flower for her. He held it out to her, his voice not a ridiculous caricature, but as elegant as a real movie star, and said, "I do believe this is for you." His expression was one of absolute tenderness, the same look you see on the face of a new parent when they hold their child for the first time. I realized for the first time why Gracie Ann loves him.

I let the window clang shut. I stood there for a long time until I heard Eddie's voice behind me.

"Feel better?" he said. I shook my head. He kissed the top of my head the way a father would kiss his child. "You need to come outside. It's too hot in here."

"I don't care." I looked up at him, quietly recounted my dream, every detail. "What do you think it means?"

"You bury your family."

Chapter 13

Wilted lettuce is a dish that needs to be served immediately. Wait too long and you'll end up with a mess. Lettuce with hot bacon grease poured over it like dressing, it congeals quickly. It is hard for most to stomach at any time with its heavy vinegar and onion taste, but it is especially difficult to swallow in the heat of summer. My old high school friends consumed it in hearty portions, laughing and talking about the high school reunion. If it isn't your loved one who has died, then funerals are not sad family reunions.

We looked the way we did in high school, the four of us huddled together, exclusively, lounging against Mama's car. They had given me "I haven't seen you in so long" hugs and condolences that could have come from a Hallmark card, but not the heart. No, the heart would require thought, and their minds were elsewhere, selfishly as always. Tiffany and Julie, blond and perky, both have nice executive jobs and live off Chenal in West Little Rock. Their lives are about order, file cabinets, and a personal parking space. Former drill team captain Tracey is a stay-at-home mom with five children, while her husband works a cushy job in "finance" (whatever that means). Politely, I paid attention to them, listening to gossip, but I felt awkward. In high school, I always "belonged." I was the leader, the head of the inner clique, but now I wanted to be with Gracie Ann, Eddie, and Jonesy as they relaxed against the tractor. I wanted to be a puzzle piece that went with another set. Jonesy had his arm around Gracie Ann's shoulder, had her pulled close, his sleeves rolled up to conquer the heat. Eddie had removed his jacket earlier when he helped me set up the food, but he had the top buttons on his shirt undone now, and his sleeves rolled up too. They looked comfortable. Friendly. I knew Gracie Ann was not happy, per se – it was Mama's funeral after all – but she was at ease in her circle with Jonesy and Eddie. They all liked each other, regardless of jobs, social standing, or bank statement. They enjoyed one another's company. I remembered what Gracie Ann had said to me about not having any real friends, only socialites. Standing with the former cheerleaders, A+ students, and homecoming court, I felt like gum on the bottom of a shoe. I was stuck somewhere I didn't belong. I was a Dunley. Chef Faith Orion was a lie. A coward. A wilted piece of lettuce served up like a fancy Southern dish. Even in the pit of the stomach, I would eventually congeal. Clog the heart.

There is an innocence in the heart of children that makes them oblivious to reality. I never had that. With scuffed dress shoes, James pushed a Tonka dump truck over to the pile of dirt Lucy was building, her little pink slippers dirty now too. The two kids had paired off, joined a clique, just like everyone there. The twins hovered on the porch over a laptop. Granny and the grandparents Orion conversed with Edward Sr., Ol' man Wilson, Bob, and Maude. The oldsters were still talking about Sears brand appliances. Granny D had the yellow flower tucked in her hair. With three fans blowing on them like whirlwinds, my aunt and two uncles were watching television inside, too young to care about quality-brand appliances, too old to send instant messages to online friends. Cousin Tootie had excused herself earlier and was probably somewhere near the Arkansas border by now.

Eddie looked nowhere close to leaving anytime soon. Always very still, calm, and serious, the only way you can gauge Eddie's emotions is by the way he moves his hands, accenting his words with a fluttering of fingers or a flick of his wrist. He keeps his emotions in wax, preserved like a bug trapped in amber. If you were able to extract it, would it fly away or would it have to be reanimated?

I looked at Tracey's plate of wilted lettuce. It could stand a quick trip to the microwave. Even in this heat, the oil from the bacon fat had started to coagulate like a big glob of drying blood.. A big lumpy mass of white goo rested on a piece of onion. How could she swallow that? I wanted to flick it off her plate in much the same way that Tiffany wanted to remove Eddie from the yard.

With a smirk, Tiffany asked, "Does he still have that garage?" They all knew who she was referring to and turned to stare at Eddie as if he were a plague, hoping he wouldn't get too close and get his cooties on them. His green handkerchief was hanging out of his pants pocket. It could just as easily have been an oil-stained rag to them.

"You know he does. What else would he be doing?" Julie replied. Ironically, she knew all about his ... cooties. She was also, allegedly, one of the naugahyde couch's reclinees.

Tracey turned to me, sweet smile. "He's still good friends with Gracie Ann after all these years. Isn't that something?" I knew what she was implying. Like a nearsighted person with new glasses, I saw clearly now. It had always been their glasses that were the wrong prescription for me.

"He's a family friend," I said and walked away.

I sat on the steps, wiping away the condensation from my glass of tea. I was the first person to see the white van with a satellite dish on the top. It pulled into the yard, even skidded a little like the van from the A-Team arriving to save the day, but these people were not there to rescue anyone.

In swift-stride, Eddie cut off Joan Commonbond, the most popular news reporter in Arkansas, before I could get inside the house. Her star was on the rise; she wanted to use my name to help secure that, in case her relationship with Pulitzer prize-winning journalist Ryan Ingram didn't make her look important enough.

My hand on the door, I heard her say, "We want to know why she didn't go to the funeral."

Granny pulled a switch from a tree. "I told you to get yer tail away from my baby's funeral and now I'm a tellin' ya to get yer behind off my property."

Eddie covered the cameraman's lens. Jonesy sauntered over, back to his extroverted showman self, and said politely but firmly, "I can understand your dilemma, being in showbiz myself ... "

"I'm not in showbiz," Joan corrected. But she is. Of the real-life kind. And far more exploitive.

"I gave you an interview already, now the lady here asked you to leave. I think you should," Jonesy said to her but it was to no avail. Joan was camping in that spot, ready for a sit-in like a college campus protesting a war.

Granny was at a loss. Her switch was not having the desired effect.

"You need to put that down," Joan said to her.

The oldsters sashaying to my Granny D's rescue captivated me. They were lost in some long-forgotten moment of chivalry. My hand grasped the door handle, but I was stuck to the porch steps like a fly in honey. I couldn't make it inside. They surrounded her like zombies from *Thriller*.

Ol' man Wilson said, "You leave Marly alone."

"This isn't about the old lady," Joan retorted, angrier now. Her hair-sprayed locks barely moved when the wind blew.

"Old?" Granny D said. Scorned and that was real bad.

"I just want to talk to Faith Orion and I'll leave," Joan said, glancing at me. She waved, friendly-like. I shook my head.

Toothless Bob said, "Leave lil' Faith alone too. She has a'right to grieve."

"But she didn't go to the funeral. Why?" Joan asked.

Grandpa Orion put his magnetism and arthritis aside. "You're not going to upset my granddaughter."

"The nerve. Bothering someone after a funeral. Have you no class?" Grandma Orion said.

Even the dog Jake wanted to get involved. He barked at Joan.

"Just let me talk to her," Joan said. "Does he bite?" No one answered. "It won't take five seconds," Joan begged, looked to me again. "Please, Faith, real quick."

"Get over it," Starry said, standing, finally leaving the comfort of the internet. "She's not going to talk to you."

"Ever," Night added, arms folded. We had bonded over the Dunley-Weston brawl and strawberry shortcake.

Gracie Ann, her arm around her husband, said to Joan, "Really, you need to leave."

Having put away his toys, and speaking again in a very adult-sounding voice, James said, "The lady has requested that you leave. Failure to do so could result in some very disastrous and dire consequences for you and your cameraman here." He looked at the cameraman, who was busy trying to get Eddie's hand off the lens. "Canon XL. Lame. You should be shooting with at least a Canon XL H1," James said.

Fed up, Granny D raised her switch to the news crew. "Get out or I'm calling the law!"

Maude put up her dukes. Her fists looked bigger than her boobs, but I didn't think they would make better weapons. Those breasts had to have once been heavy to hang that low.

"We'll fight you. Tooth and nail. We will, won't we, Maude?" Granny D said.

Joan rolled her eyes. "Are you getting this?" she asked the cameraman, but he was busy trying to get the camera back from Eddie.

Uncles John and Henry and Aunt Jane had come out on the porch now, having heard the commotion from inside. They tried to get me inside, but I still couldn't move. I couldn't believe they were all defending me this way. Faith Orion, the one who shies away from them, who fought the crazy both tooth and nail. The normal one. The one who hasn't been home in twenty years. The one who should have swallowed her medicine.

Like a doctor with the perfect remedy, take this and you'll feel better, Edward Sr. handed Joan a shiny rock. She knocked it, hard, out of his hand. The bug in amber released. Calmly, Eddie gave the camera back to the man and stood nose to nose with Joan. "Don't you ever touch my grandfather again," he said, then turned to Gracie Ann for help. "I can't hit a girl."

Before Gracie Ann could respond, Joan stepped back and said, "You're all nuts!"

"Crazy is a better word, and you better leave before you see the depths of it," I said. Everyone looked at me. The quiet one. Standing at the doorway, hand no longer glued to that door, wanting to escape. I stomped down the steps. "Leave my family alone."

"I just want a quote," Joan said, thinking I had finally come to my senses even if I was enraged.

"What you're going to get is knocked upside the jaw," I said. Granny puffed up her chest, proud. Maude kept those fists high in the air. Dunley brawls are the best.

"Do it and I'll sue," Joan said.

"Let 'em sue. I'll pay the damages, the fuckers," Granny said back, sounding like a peeved Hunter S. Thompson.

Joan huffed and said to me, "You're as crazy as the rest of them." She tapped the cameraman. "Fine," she said, "It's a simple question." She looked directly at me, angry and confused. "We are going to do a story irregardless."

"Irregardless really isn't a word," James said.

"Why didn't you go to the funeral, Faith?" Joan asked, one

last hope. A story is worth a punch in the face, worth more than the gold in Fort Knox.

"Don't you judge my sister," Gracie Ann said. "She's a good person. You mind your business."

Suddenly comprehending that this was all about me, Lucy got angry. She pushed away the toy truck. "Are you being mean to my Aunt Faith?" The little hurricane erupted again, and she kicked out a headlight on the news van.

"Mother fuc– " Joan started but Gracie Ann grabbed her before she could get the word out.

"Don't you say those words in front of my kids!" Jonesy said. His cheery demeanor broken.

Gracie Ann shoved Joan and picked up Lucy, who was hopping around in pain. I could see the drop of blood coming through the pink slipper. Everyone rushed to check on Lucy, but the news crew used the diversion to hassle me. I was more important than a possible broken toe.

"I want to check on my niece," I said, trying to move away.

"Give me one quote, and we won't sue you for that broken headlight," Joan said.

"Do what you have to do. Sue me. I don't care," I said and ran to Lucy. Before I could reach her, my high school friends, having watched the ordeal with the same rapt amusement but for different reasons, came up to me. They each made their excuses for leaving, and I saw Tiffany give Joan a business card. They all sped away, grateful to be away from the crazy Dunleys.

Granny chased the news truck out of the yard, and Lucy's foot turned out to be fine, only a little cut from the broken glass. James was livid, just livid that his betrothed had been injured in the scuffle. He sat next to her the rest of the day, holding her hand and feeding her apple pie. Her foot had a little bandage just like the cut on his hand.

"Apples are medicinal," he said, as if it were true, as I sat next to them on the porch steps and watched.

Everyone else reveled in the event as if it were a story on the five o'clock news, which I knew it would be, like Joan said, with or without a quote from me.

Eddie came over and sat beside me. "I was right. You Dunleys are always up for a good fight."

I smirked. "There was no fight."

"Almost," he said, rolling a smoke.

"I can't believe I did that." I put my face in my hands.

"Retrospect," Eddie said, taking a puff from his cigarette, "is our greatest gift and our greatest failing."

"Are you saying I should have decked her?" I said, looking up at him.

"Should have, but that's not what I meant." The cigarette dangled in his right hand, waiting for another puff. "We can always look back on things and see meaning, see gifts, remember things fondly, see all types of important moments and lessons. We get it later, you know, understand it, which is a blessing. But we don't have the chance to change it, if it needed correcting, or appreciate it at the time it took place, which is a shame."

I took a sip of tea, tried to stay focused on the tire swing blowing in the slight breeze. "I feel bad enough. I should have gone to the funeral. I know that." I turned to look at him. "Don't make me feel worse, please."

"I'm not. I wouldn't do that to you." He placed his left hand gently on my knee.

James took his plate of apple pie, and Lucy's hand, and they walked down the steps. "They need to be alone," James whispered to her.

"He's very adult for a boy," I said to Eddie, patting his hand.

Eddie jerked his hand away and ran it quickly through his hair. "He's a strange cookie."

"Can't imagine where he gets it," I said in way of a friendly jab, feeling awkward now too.

"Oh, I think we know where he gets it," he said, taking one last puff, flicking his cigarette in the yard. He made a quick glance over to Edward Sr.

"He gave me a shiny rock too. What does it mean? What's the symbolism?"

Eddie made a little chuckle, the edges of his mouth almost a full smile. "He collects shiny rocks. Thinks they're pretty."

"They don't have some deep mystical meaning?"

"Nah. He's just nuts. He's the *strangest* cookie." Eddie made a swirly motion with his finger near his temple to show craziness. "But I love him anyway."

I looked away, then looked around, looked at the collection of people in the yard, the place I grew up, the place that was as familiar to me as the back of my hand. I knew every vein, every line, every crease. Of course I did. It was mine. I couldn't cut it off anymore than I could my hand.

"You can still go," Eddie said, standing.

I held out my hand, wanting him to help me stand. For a moment, he hesitated then took my hand in his. It was soft, not calloused. I felt everyone's eyes on me as we walked to Eddie's truck, but they weren't judging or suspicious. Before she had left, Tracey had placed her unfinished plate of wilted lettuce on top of the trash can. It was an oily, glumpy mess – green pieces like snot covered in mucous. Desirable to no one. I picked it up and dumped it inside the trash can where it belonged.

The summer heat had melted me, but I was not wilted lettuce. Not anymore. I was ready to say goodbye to my mother, to make amends with my family. I was ready to feel the breeze as it came in from the rolled-down window of Eddie's truck.

Chapter 14

The window rolled down, I took in the scent of mulberries and watched the fields go by. One after another, the fields. Some barren. Some freshly plowed. Some with bounty. I looked at Eddie. He was looking at something in the rearview mirror. I looked back; I saw nothing, just the stretch of road behind us. Ahead of us, more fields. Eddie was in a field when I first met him at age five. He had stuck a raw cotton puff in my hair from a plant that was the last of a long-forgotten crop in the field. I had been trespassing in his yard and picking flowers, skipping and singing some song (who knows what now). I saw that little boy in the distance, running over to me. With unruly windswept hair, his first words ever to me had been, "You're a girl." He popped off the cotton puff and put it in my hair. "Girls wear flowers," he had said, authoritative, sure that he was right. "That's not a flower," I had said back and pushed him hard. My girlish shoe stomped it into the ground. "This is a flower," I had said, holding up one I had been picking in his yard. Unflustered, he had examined it, then said the strangest of things.

In the truck, I looked over at Eddie and repeated it to him. "Roses are red, I say they are blue."

"What?" he said with a chuckle, the same chuckle he always has that resides in his chest and never makes it all the way out.

"You said that to me when we were kids. Do you remember?"

He shook his head.

"I was picking flowers on your property. You put a cotton puff in my hair ... "

Remembering, he said, "You stomped it! I was so mad."

"You didn't act mad. You got all philosophical," I replied, lightheartedly.

"You'd still stomp it."

"But you said that, about the flowers being blue, that they could be anything, just pretend. The cotton puff could be a flower. I remember that."

"You wanted real flowers." He said it almost forlorn, like someone who realized they could only give faux diamonds, never real gems, to the one they loved.

The Field property was always untamed when I was growing up. They did not plant any crops, rarely mowed the yard, and various car parts and junk stacked up everywhere. Gracie Ann loved it. She called it "The Jungle." She spent many days with Eddie climbing on rusted tractors, hiding in tall grasses, and snaking through rotting tires.

"You want to know what's ironic?" Eddie asked, again glancing in his rearview mirror before looking at me. "You picked weeds."

"They were wildflowers."

"Weeds. They look like flowers, but technically they're weeds."

Anyone can tell a corn stalk just by looking at it. It always looks the same, but there is a fine line between a weed and a flower.

"Still pretty," I replied.

"Faith Orion decorating her house with weeds. For shame."

"They can be flowers if I say so."

"Like a cotton puff?"

"Like a cotton puff." Begrudgingly.

"What's that? What's that?" he joked, getting in my face.

"Just watch the road, Eddie."

"You are a strange cookie." He stared at me, half-smile, but there was a shift in his vision this time. He still had the same serious expression as always, but he was like a child looking through a View-Master toy, the image changed with a CLICK. He looked for a moment, observed the scene, then CLICK ... but he glanced at the rearview again. What was back there that he kept looking at? The projector jammed; he wouldn't click to the next frame, so I narrated the scene for him.

"The Toltec Mounds," I pointed out. I could see them up ahead. Unlike the hilltop at Mulberry Pointe, these are real Native American grounds built over one thousand years ago by the Plum Bayou people. Of the remaining mounds, one is considered a burial mound. Granny tells a story about visiting the Toltec Mounds as a child. The wind had swept up her dress, exposing herself to no one, she says, except the breeze. That cooling wind flicked the leaves and the limbs of a nearby mulberry tree. She plucked a berry and ate it. No one had ever planted that tree, you reckon, but there it was waiting for its berries to be jam some day. It's still there, that tree, but some day it will be gone. Someone will cut it down, or it will die from old age, its berries all carried off in pasteurized jars of jam. Over time, the mounds will erode, too. Be gone, only a memory, the past. Just like Mama's body which resides not far from the mounds. The field is the only thing that never fades. That's the thing about a piece of land, it can never leave. A strong foundation, the starting point for everything, but land is at the mercy of whatever is planted in, or placed upon, its soil. Nurturing or housing whatever you ask, they accept this fate. They are fields.

Accepting Mama's death may never truly come to me, but she belongs in this place, a foundation for new growth. Part of the landscape. Part of my past. I spent my life trying to run far away from her, to excel in everything she did not, looking back at her with a smirk like Eddie glancing in that rearview mirror. What was back there that I kept staring at? She never sneered back; she just kept walking. My entire family kept walking even though I had become a tiny spec far ahead on the horizon. I was the one who had to keep looking over my shoulder. Reassured, they were still there. No matter how far I ran, how quickly, they remained.

Mama had finally stopped walking but I could still see her. Eddie touched my shoulder gently, as we reached Ironton Cemetery. He pulled into the lot, shifted the truck into park, and the grinding of the gears sounded so final. He looked at me. Time to get out. My legs forgot how to move forward, as I stood on the hot pavement. Like moving through a jungle of tall grasses, I maneuvered just as slowly to the family plot of graves.

I put my hand on the fresh mound of dirt. Cold, not hot from the summer heat. Mama's headstone: Karen Dunley-Orion. I touched it. Cold too. There were so many flowers. Those would not stay forever, but Mama would. Lingering in the air. I would return to Boston.

"I'll leave you alone," Eddie said to me and walked to another row of graves marked "Field." There were no fresh flowers on the grave he visited, but there were some dried ones, not old though, recently deceased. It looked like a handwritten note was attached, a child's drawing on notebook paper.

I turned back to Mama, imagining her ears were like that cotton puff. Who is to say for certain that your ears stop working after you die? "I did everything right," I finally said, quietly, fidgeting, hoping no one else could hear. "I was perfect. I really did think that, Mama, that I could protect you if I was perfect." I fidgeted again. "Obsessive-compulsive, that's what it's called. Granny D would be so proud of my style of crazy. Don't get me wrong, I'm not embracing any crazy." Death doesn't stop punch lines, but what does one say to a headstone? To a mound of dirt?

To my left, I cautiously glanced beside Mama's grave. Charles Orion. A few fresh flowers were placed on his grave. I knew those were from Gracie Ann and the grandparents Orion. I took some more from Mama's plot and put them on Dad's grave. I knew she wouldn't mind. "How are things, Dad? I'm grown now. Did you ever meet the Field boy? No, I don't guess you did. Eddie Jr., the mechanic's grandson. You'd like him. He fixes things too." Talking to my father felt even weirder. I only have one flash of memory from his funeral. Click, not like a View-Master, but a blinding light like a flashbulb going off too soon. I remember the feel of Mama's hand on the day of Dad's funeral. Soft. Not clammy, cold, or any other cliche of how a hand might feel on a dead day. No. Just soft. A mother's hand.

Looking to my right at Poppy D's grave, I said, "Did you know I got married? Yeah, in France. Granny D probably told you. She talks to you all the time. I'm divorced now. I have a cooking show ... Mama can tell you more about – " All words ceased abruptly. Retrospect, like Eddie had said. I couldn't change it, and it seemed very pointless to try. "This is stupid," I said to myself, feeling like an idiot.

I felt Eddie's hand on my back. "No, it's not," he said.

"They can't hear, Eddie." I looked at him, hoping he could give me redemption as if he were a god. If my life were an Egyptian myth, Eddie could resurrect my loved ones and let me have one last word before they floated off to the stars. They would become the night sky and guide me whenever I looked up. Instead, I looked down, down to the ground that my mother's body resided in.

Tears don't really rush out in torrents, or floods, or any manner of wild adjectives. Emotions do, but not tears, per se. They always roll out slowly. They build behind the eyes, then slide out without permission. I saw one of the tears wet the ground. My face was streaked but calm when I asked, "I don't even know what to say to them."

He sat on his knees next to Mama's grave, took my hand, and pulled me to the ground. "You can say 'wado'," he replied. "It's Cherokee. It means 'thank you'." Still holding my hand, he pressed it into the dirt, then made me look at it. "I don't know what you believe, Faith, but your mother is not this dirt. Don't let it scare you, seeing this pile of earth here. She's not buried. She's still with you, just different."

He wiped away the soil from my palm. His hands are soft too. Taking out the green handkerchief from his pocket, he got close to wipe the tears from my cheeks, his lips pursed like always, like he is about to kiss. Like a bird catching a slight movement of something in the grass, his gaze shifted. Back to the graves marked "Field." He put his hands on my arms, helped me stand up.

We started to walk back to the truck and I asked, referring to Mindy Field, "Is that what you say to her? Wado?"

There was a very slight ripple over his face before he answered, "No. To her I say 'I'm sorry'."

"Sorry for what?"

He just smiled, sadly.

I went back and took a flower from one of Mama's bouquets. "She can have one of Mama's," I said, handing him a flower. "She should have a fresh one."

"I put some there last week," he said, tugging my arm.

We walked back to the truck. Back inside, windows still down, he fumbled around in his pocket. "I need a smoke." He took out a pack, tapped it two times on the dashboard, and stuck a cigarette in his mouth.

"I thought you rolled your own?" I said as he pulled out a lighter and lit the cigarette.

"All out. Gotta make do."

Eddie put the car in gear; it rolled backwards easily. He looked in the rearview for obstacles, something that might impede our leaving. Nothing there. He yanked on the gear; it didn't want to click into the forward position. His perpetual cool breaking a little, he smacked his hand against the steering wheel, and we moved.

As we traveled back the way we had arrived, passing it all again, I said, "She thought I hated her. My mom."

"Why do you think that?"

"I did sometimes."

"We all hate our parents at times. That's normal."

"I was always mean to her, criticized her. I shouldn't have."

With his serious look painted on like a mask, he said, "Don't start thinking she hated you. No parent hates their child."

"You know more about my family than I do."

"That's not true. You've just lost touch." He looked at me, those eyes that look like they have been dipped in a fertile valley, a dark green harvest.

"Eddie, you've done too much for my family. Just too much. I don't know how to repay you." I grinned. "Wado."

The sun was starting to set. I didn't realize so much time had passed. In the distance, in my memories, I saw little Eddie running towards me. I moved too, and a twig snapped under my feet. He was no longer a boy. He was a man, his field vast, open. The big oak tree in Granny D's yard was a fledgling, newly planted. Gracie Ann had been right all along. A new one did emerge. I sat down next to it, rooted myself to that spot. Eddie put a cotton puff in my hair. A yellow flower. It was time for it to grow.

Chapter 15

Look at any field, you see the dirt, you see the vegetables, you see the blue sky. I used to think Eddie Field was in full bloom, full view, easy to pick out the parts that were stems, the parts that were seeds, the parts ready to harvest. But with Eddie, hidden beneath the soil is a quiet part of him. He raises his son, takes care of mothers dying of lupus, and teaches eager children about literature. He nurtures. There is also a piece of him that is upturned like new dirt ready for seeds, a thirst for something to be planted in him. He reads novels, learns about mysticism, and plays guitar. He feeds himself. When we went to visit my mother's grave, I found the neglected part, a piece of earth left to grow wild with weeds. Was it unusable? Or castoff and forgotten? Did he know it was there? If he looked far enough, would he see the giant oak tree with new leaves, sturdy bark, and cool shade? Did he want to? It begged for someone to be near it, a branch swaying in a breeze like a hand held out. I wanted to sit underneath it, be near it, rest my head, pull my legs up to me, and just be there ...

"You're on the filter, babe," Eddie said to me, my first cigarette burned to nothing. I flicked it out the window, coming out of my daydream.

"Still with us?" Gracie Ann asked. We were all on our way to a folk dancing lesson. Piled into Jonesy's rented SUV, Gracie Ann was in the passenger seat, while I sat next to Eddie. James and Lucy were in the very back cargo area situated face-to-face like luggage, drinking up the last of their Sonic malts. The twins had opted to stay home with Granny D. Their two favorite music groups, Hott Stuf and Tres, were performing live on MTV. Granny agreed, they couldn't miss that. Besides, it was nice and cool in the house now. Eddie and Jonesy had already installed a new central air unit.

The other relatives had all gone home, wherever that might be for them. The rest of us enjoyed the night air, which was a little unseasonably cool, as it blew into the SUV's open windows. I'm not sure why I decided to try a smoke, other than the fact it had been between Eddie's pursed perfect lips. When he offered me a taste, I obliged. I had choked, wheezed, and turned various shades of red and blue, but I held it in my mouth. I was cool. When he had given me a small kiss on the cheek after taking me home from the grave site, I was nonchalant then too. Inside, a thousand lovelorn sappy overly-romantic sweep-me-off-my-feet silly thoughts had rushed around in my head all night. I felt guilty. Mama. When I thought about Mama being dead, though, the soured beans taste wasn't as strong anymore. At two o'clock in the morning, I had gotten out of bed, fixed myself a giant plate of purple hull peas, and ate them in the moonlight. Orion had looked back at me. He was a hunter. He had a bow and an arrow and his trusty dogs. If he aimed just right, I bet he always hit his mark. I had smiled and hoped my family, resting somewhere up there peacefully, had found what they had always been looking for too.

Driving through Mulberry Field, my thoughts flickering in and out of daydreams like channels changing on a television, I could see the brightest star in the sky, Sirius, through the open car window. It held itself high above Mulberry Pointe and Granny's favorite pajama-flyin' flagpole. There was nothing atop it, but it was not a lonely, empty, left-over hill of dirt. The tip of Orion's arrow pointed toward it.

"I can't believe they arrested Granny for flying her pajamas," I said and playfully nudged Eddie. "She was doing a jig *you* taught her, an Indian mourning dance."

"Lordy. Is that what she said?" Nervously, he tapped his fingers on the seat. Gracie Ann cleared her throat.

"What?" I asked.

Gracie Ann leaned back to look at me. "They didn't really arrest her, Faith. They brought her in to console her. She had a breakdown like she did after the funeral." She said this all in a whisper so the kids wouldn't hear. "They couldn't calm her down. Eddie went down ... "

"I picked her up at the station, helped her get some sleep, that's all," Eddie said, feeling uncomfortable taking credit.

"Eddie's the one who made the funeral arrangements."

"You did all that?"

He shrugged.

"There's no way she could have done it herself," Gracie Ann said. "When Eddie called me, she was a wreck."

Eddie had called Gracie Ann; I got the news from a secretary. Before I came home for Mama's funeral, the idea of seeing all my relatives had made me feel like a puzzle piece in the wrong set. After being home awhile, it felt like I had been a lost piece, hiding somewhere in a corner, accidentally knocked out of the box. But, Eddie, he was a scattered million mini tiny pieces. He was all over the place. He needed to be put back together, but no matter how hard I examined the picture, there was that missing piece in his puzzle too.

"Wado," I said to Eddie, remembering my new word.

"What's that?" Gracie Ann asked. He had never taught it to her. Smug and happy, I explained it to her, all my insides gushing around like warm liquid, making me blush.

"She really likes you, Eddie," Gracie Ann said. I thought my skin turned crimson like the bottom of a ceramic teapot left on the stove too long. Everyone could see my contents spilling all over. "Granny does. We all do too," she added with a warm smile, reached back and patted his leg, then shot me a sneaky look. She knew I was as pink as Lucy's ballet slippers.

"Granny D tolerates me, I think," he said. "I don't know why."

"I think we all tolerate her. Granny is a handful," Gracie Ann said.

"Hot tamales and get your lemons! I love her. She keeps me energized," Jonesy said, excited as always. "She's great. Yeah, really really great. I wish my granny had been like her."

"She's a crack up," Eddie replied.

"I've never seen you 'crack up'," I said. "Have you guys ever noticed that? You only do this little sly smile thing, barely raising the corners of your mouth." I mimicked his expression. "I've never seen you really laugh out loud."

"You know she's right," Gracie Ann said.

"Ha!" Eddie said in way of correcting me. "How was that?"

"Not good at all," I replied.

"Terrible," Gracie Ann said.

"Damn."

James jumped into the conversation. "Some people can't laugh. Their facial muscles are misaligned. It's a real disease," he said with a final slurp of his chocolate malt.

"Your dad can't smile?" Lucy asked, a tinge of sadness in her voice.

"I can smile, Lucy," Eddie said to her, tapped her knee, and smiled at her.

"That was a very fake smile," I said to be annoying.

"I know how to make Dad laugh," James told us. "He likes to be tickled– "

"Okay, that's enough," Eddie said to him.

"Do tell, James," Gracie Ann said, leaning around in her seat. "Where does you father like to be tickled?" She leaned far back, tried to tickle Eddie's stomach, but he grabbed her wrist.

"Tomato Puddin', leave Eddie alone," Jonesy said.

Gracie Ann yanked her wrist back. "I bet it's his feet."

Eddie raised an eyebrow. "Oh, what a shame, there's the barn. We're here. Time for a little dancin','" Eddie said, looked at me, and produced a row of perfectly shiny teeth housed in a very exaggerated smile.

The barn was lit up like a harvest ball. We all piled out of the SUV, went inside, and expected to see Southern belles and gentleman callers. What we saw were hippies, older men in Dockers, and women with T-shirts that said "Wicca." Up on stage was a simple band – a banjo player, guitarist, and a guy with thinning hair playing the dulcimer. People milled around, drank punch, and conversed.

"You don't strike me as the folk dancing type," I said to Eddie.

He thumbed over to James, who was already teaching Lucy and Gracie Ann a few steps. "He likes it."

Jonesy had already made friends, worked the place like a Hollywood mixer. He gave out his card, waved those hands in the air, and looked around the room in amazement. "Hot tamales and get your lemons! Yeah," I heard him say, "This would make a great set-up for my next picture. You see, there are villains, alien villains, and they crash land right here, inside this barn, make it their base camp." He held both hands up like looking through a camera lens. "I could shoot a picture show here. Yeah. Who do I talk to about renting this barn? I could make a whole picture here ... "

"I'm afraid he's serious," I said to Eddie.

"Frightening."

"Not as frightening as folk dancing. I can't believe I let you all talk me into this."

"It's not hard. You want me to show you some steps?" Before

I could answer, he took both my hands. "It's a mix of square dancing and line dancing. Very easy. They'll explain each dance before we start, then we jump in." He spun me around a few times. The room seemed to spin as if I were drunk. "Dosado and such." He pulled me a little closer, moved slower, his hip pressed into mine, dipped me back real fast. We must have looked like a scene in Lucy's favorite movie, *Dirty Dancing*, the way our bodies moved in sync. Wee Ste-fan never liked to dance. He always held me at arms length and never moved. Come to think of it, that's also how Stephan made love. My head rested under Eddie's chin; I felt him move against me. I wanted to be a piece of wax. Stick a wick in me; I wanted to be on fire.

Gracie Ann sauntered over and made a little kissing noise in my ear. "Nice moves, sis." Eddie pulled back, nodded, very cool. "That's just some of the moves, steps," he said, looking around. "You want something to drink?"

I shook my head. I furrowed my brow at Gracie Ann as she made her way over to her husband, who was still cooking up a whale of a Hollywood deal with the Wiccan barn owner. I could tell she was mouthing "K-I-S-S-I-N-G" in my direction, doing a little jig to accompany it. "Stop it," I mouthed back, looked at Eddie who was getting punch for the kids. "You wanna kiss him," I could tell she said. I made a slice across my neck with my finger. "Ooh, so scared," she said back across the room.

I walked over to her. "Just cool it," I said.

"Would you kiss him already and get it over with," she whispered back. "You know you want to."

"Gracie ... "

"Kissy kissy."

The dulcimer player tapped the microphone and everyone looked up. Eddie and the kids joined us. "James, would it be all right if I had the first dance with Lucy?" Eddie asked.

"It is customary for the father to have one dance with the bride," James said, thought about it, then added, "It's okay." James took my hand. Yes, it was all very cute, but I couldn't help but feel a little hurt by Eddie's decision. Gracie Ann shrugged and shook her head; she didn't understand either.

Step one, step two, step three ... we all lined up, men on one side, women on the other. Facing each other, the music started. James took my arm in his, in the course of the dance, I ended up with Eddie. Did he know that was going to happen? Throughout the evening, we always ended up in each other's arms, but I also had the misfortune to dance with Jonesy, who moves like a jumping bean and makes up his own steps when he misses a beat. He wasn't as bad as the man, in mid-dosey or mid-doe, who asked, "Are you Faith Orion? I watch your show all the time. Can you write some of your recipes down for me?" But Eddie rescued me. I always came back to Eddie. He hooked his arm in mine, around we went ...

Round two. By the time we arrived back home, we were all giddy, but things weren't so chipper at Granny D's house. There had been another Weston incident.

"I didn't want that boy dating my baby, but I certainly didn't want him breakin' her heart," Granny said, livid. She punched the air. None of us wanted Granny in another fist fight, but we were all upset to hear what had happened. "The boy," as Granny D called him, had sent Starry a text message asking her to sneak out for "some fun," insinuating a sexual encounter. Jonesy's cheerful demeanor soured; his face went stone cold, his brow furrowed, and "FATHER" emerged, squashing B-movie director like a genuine multiple personality taking over to rescue the weaker being on the outside. "She's twelve," he said, teeth clenched. Jonesy might not have been born into the Dunley bloodline, but he is one at heart. Always up for a good fight. Gracie Ann's fists were balled up at her side. Before Night could recount the rest of the tale, Eddie took Lucy and James outside.

"Starry told him she's not *that* kind of girl," Night said.

"That's my girl," Gracie Ann said.

"They could make out and that was all," Night added.

"Uh! You're too young to be making out," Gracie Ann exclaimed. "You're lucky I don't ground the both of you. I told you not to hang out with those ... "

"Westons." Granny said it like she had just thrown up a pile of rotted boiled cabbage.

"What did I tell you two?" Gracie Ann said. It was weird to see her playing the "Mom" role so well.

"Mom!" Night said, trying to explain the story. "What'd I do?"

"Let her finish," Jonesy said, still stoned faced, wanting an excuse to knock out a Weston.

Being a Weston and having no moral code, "the boy" had replied with a hateful email, saying Starry's bloodlines were dirty, her Granny made soured jam, and her Cali accent was lame. Jonesy smacked his fist against his palm. Fracas time.

Eddie was tickling the kids when the three of us – Jonesy, Gracie Ann, and I – went outside. His playfulness stopped when he saw our faces.

"There's going to be a rumble," Gracie Ann said, mocking a 1950s hoodlum.

"Kids, go inside. Granny D will get you some Fizz soda," Eddie said to them.

"Fizz fizz, that's the bizz," James sang. "I love Fizz. How 'bout you, mizz?" Lucy giggled and they ran indoors.

"Dunleys always up for a good fight," Eddie said to the rest of us.

"There will be no fight!" I said.

Jonesy rolled up his sleeves. "I want revenge. Yeah. Revenge. That'll show 'em, messing with our little girl, eh, Tomato Puddin'?"

"Let's do it. You in, Eddie?" Gracie Ann asked.

He nodded. "What do you have in mind?"

"Look, no fighting. We've done that already. Can't we ... "

"Faith, you in or out?" Gracie Ann asked, livid. "That's my daughter, the punk! I could just smash his little face in!"

Eddie sucked the inside of his cheek, thought about it, and said, "Let's toilet paper the place."

Rubbing his hands together like a 1930s gangster, Jonesy exclaimed, "Egg it! Let's egg it too!"

"Rockin'," Eddie said.

"And cut off that boy's little dick," Jonesy added.

So there it was. The big plan, minus the dick-cutting part. We got back into the SUV and rolled over to Ruthie Weston's. Cut our headlights a few feet from her house. The lights were all off in her house, too. Quiet. Too quiet for Jonesy's liking.

"You think it could be booby trapped?" he asked, having made too many movies to see the world rationally.

"I'm stealing the jelly," Gracie Ann said, getting out of the car and taking a case of jelly from the steps. "We'll dump it in a river or something."

"What river?" I asked in a whisper, as Eddie and Jonesy took out a giant package of toilet paper.

"The Arkansas River. I'm not eating it. You want to eat this crap?"

I shook my head and took a roll of toilet paper. I looked at Eddie. "I don't know how."

"Just throw it and let it roll, babe," he said, chucking one into a tree.

Something happened to me as I watched that roll of white cottony tissue sail through the air like a fat streamer. Mischief. I had never made mischief before. The tissue went into the tree, wrapped over a few limbs, and landed with a thud back on the ground. I tore off the end, unrolled what was left and threw it. Mischief. I started laughing. Eddie just shook his head at me. He had an amazing ability to make his TP loop several limbs before toppling back to the ground.

"You've done this before," I said.

"Many a time," he answered.

Jonesy moved onto the eggs. He splattered the front porch, the walls, even a few trees. Gracie Ann drew a picture on a jar of strawberry jelly and left it near the front door. I'm too much of a lady to describe it, but it referred to "the boy's" genitalia in a most unflattering way.

A light flicked on inside the house.

"Hot tamales and get your lemons! The jig is up," Jonesy yelled, holding an egg. He threw it, hitting Ruthie's boney chest when she opened the door.

We all ran back to the SUV, but Jonesy slipped on the ground. Gracie Ann went back for him, but it was too late. Ruthie and her brood were coming down the porch steps, hollering and cussing. Jonesy did what any man would do in this situation. He dropped his trousers and mooned the lot of 'em. Unfortunately, Jonesy is not familiar with the proper way to moon someone. He stood there, full-frontal nude, his "Jonesy" dangling in front of a startled old lady.

That's when I heard Eddie laugh. A full-on belly laugh doubled over in hysterics.

Jonesy and Gracie jumped back in the car. We sped off with Westons waving their fists at us like angry, dumbfounded, Keystone coppers. Luckily none of the men waved anything else at us. That would have been a blinding sight.

"Man, that was great!" Jonesy said.

"Let's do something wild. I'm energized," Gracie Ann added.

"Eddie, you all right?" I asked, because he was still laughing, his eyes watering. He waved his hand at me, but couldn't stop chuckling.

Through muffled laughter, he said, "Did you see Ruthie's face?"

"It was more gnarled than usual," I replied.

Eddie laughed more. If you didn't know he was laughing, you would have thought he was choking. He could barely breathe. He leaned over to me, whispered in my ear, "That's not the only thing that's ... " He broke off. "I can't. I can't," he said only to me, quietly. I knew what he meant and leaned on his shoulder, giggling myself.

"No, seriously, y'all. Let's do something," Gracie Ann said. "Get naked and go skinny dipping."

Eddie was seriously doubling over in pain. "Oh, I think one of us already got naked," he was able to say. My legs were curled up next to me. My stomach hurt from laughing.

Gracie Ann, ignoring us, said, "Come on, let's do something crazy wild."

"Let's rob someone," Jonesy suggested.

Eddie stopped laughing. A pin could have dropped. We all looked at Jonesy.

"What?" Jonesy said.

We all broke out into laughter.

"What? What? You know I was joking!" Jonesy said, but we weren't listening anymore.

Silliness can make you do the strangest of things. Like go skinny dipping. Not far from the Weston property is a place called Old Rice Creek. There used to be a rice farm many years ago, and the only remains are a mill and a creek that was the main irrigation source on the land. It was a popular spot when I was a teenager for skinny dipping and school skipping.

We weren't ditching class, but we looked like a few kids up to no good. We had stopped off at a liquor store and sat in the car getting drunk off cheap whiskey. It still tasted better than Tag's liquor. I've never been much for whiskey, so I was loopy before anyone else. As adult people, we knew it was unsafe to jump into a creek stone cold drunk, but we did it anyway. Adults. Acting like kids. Mischief. Gracie Ann and Jonesy were the first in the water, splashing around like idiots. I don't think either of them really needed liquor; they were still high on our night of mischief. Cool even when inebriated, Eddie took off his clothes slowly. Drunk, and I couldn't bring myself to do it, even on a night of mischief.

Putting his shirt on the hood of the car, Eddie looked at me and said, "Go in the woods there and do it. No one will look."

Shyly, I did what he said. My back was to everyone as I undid my blouse. I could hear Gracie Ann and Jonesy sloshing about. One button. Two. Then I felt Eddie's hands over mine. Three.

Eddie does not make love in any way, drunk or no, like Wee Ste-fan. Granny D had said Stephan was not a full-sized man. If she only knew that could be implied in more ways than one. Eddie, well, I wouldn't use the word "wee" to describe him other than to say "we" made love like wild crazy insane oblivious-to-everyone in-bliss animals. I found that secret part of Eddie that had been neglected for too long, because he came like a priest who had been given a "get laid free" card by God himself. It was like we had found the oasis of sex in a dry desert that we had both been bumbling around in for too long. At some point, we did notice that Gracie Ann and Jonesy had gotten real quiet. They weren't in the water. They were doing it too.

Chapter 16

There was a drunk afterglow haze that surrounded all of us as we got back to the car. No one said anything on the way back, although a chuckle rippled through all of us when we passed the Weston home, TP still hanging from the trees.

Granny was still awake; she had pulled out the sofa bed, tucked all four kids inside, sound asleep. She sat at the kitchen table, didn't mention our wet bodies, our disheveled clothes. We recounted the tale. When she laughed, she coughed a lot.

"Are you okay, Granny?" I asked, my thoughts leaving my romp in the thicket.

"I'm fine, fine," she said. But she didn't seem fine. Her face was very red. "Just get me some water."

"You need a doctor?" Gracie Ann asked.

"Hell, no! What's wrong with you?" She stomped over to the faucet, poured a glass. "The lot of you, get a shower. You all smell like sex."

Before anyone could move, I saw it. A large mammoth enormous black waterbug. It twitched its long antenna at me, frozen but cocky, knowing it could outrun me. Calmly, but wanting to shriek, I said, "Eddie, there's a bug."

Gracie Ann looked back; it was near her foot. She did what I wanted to do – yell like the house were on fire. So did Jonesy. Being from L.A., the only large vermin he knows are Hollywood executives. Nonchalant, Eddie picked up the roach with his bare hands. Everyone, except Granny D, reeled back, ridiculously afraid he might ask us to pet it.

"Just a bug. Nothing to be afraid of," he said. Granny opened the door. Eddie let the bug free. We all heard it scuttle away.

In bed that night, everyone asleep, I stared up at my ceiling, the big hole I put there from once trying to kill the very same type of bug. Throughout my entire life I had been trying to squash things I didn't like with a broom, but it always left a big hole. The one on the ceiling always seemed enormous. If I ever had a sleep-over at Granny D's with a school friend, I was so embarrassed at how tacky it looked. Thinking back on my adventures earlier in the evening, the mischief, the thicket romp, I felt warm, I felt whole, so what was the problem? Why did that hole stare back at me? There was no bug. Eddie got rid of it. I stood up on my bed, ran my finger along the crack. It was not very deep. It could be mended. I bet Eddie knows how to spackle things. If another bug bothered me, Eddie could sweep it out the door.

There was a rustling in the living room, and I heard Granny coughing in her room. I hopped out of bed, peeked out the door. James was up. Being so used to his little adult-sounding voice, it was weird to see him standing there, rubbing his eyes with the back of his hands. He looked so small. Granny coughed again.

"James," I said. "Are you all right?"

He came down the hall, looked up at me. "Where's my dad?"

I put my hand on his shoulder. "He didn't want to wake you, so he let you sleep over. Have you ever had a sleep-over before?"

He shook his head. "Can I have a drink of water?"

Kids really ask this stuff. I smiled and nodded. "You want to sleep in my room?"

"Mmmm ... are *you* scared?" he asked.

"I am a little."

"Okay," he said.

Granny coughed again. "Let's check on Granny first." I knocked on the door, James' hand in mine, and carefully peeked inside. "Granny, are you okay? You want a drink?"

"Tag's whiskey."

"No whiskey."

"Can I have whiskey too?" James asked. "A whiskey sour."

"No." I stared at him. "How do you know ... never mind."

We went to the kitchen. It was like a Jonesy movie come to life. Flying around in the kitchen, like butterflies mind you, were two very large, even larger than before, waterbugs. James screamed, jumped behind me. I put my arms out, as if that could protect either of us. They were *flying*! I didn't know they could do that! I needed Granny D's help. I couldn't do it without her.

"Granny!" I yelled. "Granny!" If she killed the bug, she could have all the whiskey she wanted. Just kill it! Where was Eddie when you needed him?

James and I backed out of the kitchen, slow-like so as not to make any sudden movements and alert the insects to our presence. We bumped into Starry, curious about the commotion. When she saw it, she went pale.

"Crap! What are those?" she asked, running back to the couch and jumping under the covers. Lucy and Night were awake now too. Without having to see anything, just from the sheer terror of the rest of us, they started screaming. They got BIG just from our reaction.

"What's all this?" Granny D said, her voice hoarse. She stood in the hallway silhouetted by the light coming from the open door of her bedroom. It made her look like an angel. "Oh good grief," she said, going into the kitchen. "Is that all?" She grabbed the broom, while the rest of us huddled together, ready to bolt if one of those creatures headed our way. With the broom, Granny swatted both bugs, knocking them to the floor and squashed them quickly. Smack, smack! Both gone. She scooped them up with the dust pan. Then she got herself a drink of water. "Faith, you can't kill a bug? You're going to have to do this stuff yourself." She took a drink. Went back to bed.

Once the children were back on the couch bed, James with me, I looked up at the ceiling again. James was looking too. "How'd that crack get there?" he asked.

"Ironically, trying to kill a bug. I missed." I sat up on my arm, looked down at him. "You don't strike me as the type to be scared of bugs."

"Mmmm ... I'm not really scared. I was just pretending," he answered.

"Me too."

He smiled. I cuddled against him, put my arm around him. I saw him eyeing Beary Gordy. "You want to hold him?" I asked. "His name is Beary Gordy."

"Berry Gordy is the founder of Motown Records."

I got up and brought the bear back to him. "Well, this one is a cuddly bear. I've had him forever."

James played with him for a little while, then asked, "Can we call my dad?"

"Now?" I asked.

"He's probably still up. He likes to meditate at night."

"How 'bout we wait 'til morning, okay?"

"Mmmm ... how 'bout we call him now?"

"You want to go home?"

"Dad and Papa might be scared without me. I always sleep with my dad. Papa sleeps in the other room. They might be worried."

"I think they'll be all right." I snuggled up against him. "When I was little and had a bad dream, my mom used to sing to me."

"Okay."

"Okay?"

"Sing me a song. Something like jump blues. Something rockin'. I like stuff like that."

"I can't sing."

"Oh."

"Granny used to make me buttered skillet toast in the middle of the night, but I can't make that very well either."

"But you're a chef."

"I know. Go figure. Hmmm, I don't want to wake Granny D for toast. She's quiet now, not coughing. I want her to get some sleep."

"What can you do?" he asked, eyes looking up to me, not acting so adult as he once did.

I thought about it. I can't kill bugs. I can't even get my grandmother a drink of water in the middle of the night. I can make beef bourguignonne, but that wouldn't do me much good. "Not much, James, not much at all."

"That's okay." He cuddled as close as he could. "Don't fall asleep. Stay awake."

"Awake, I can do that."

"You're soft. You smell nice."

"Go to sleep."

"How come you don't have any kids?"

"James, sleep, now."

"I'm going to have some kids when I grow up. A billion maybe. They'll have a mom like you. If my wife dies, you can be their mom if you want, since you don't have any kids. Will you be their mom?"

I had never heard anything that heartbreaking come out of a child's mouth. I had just lost my mother, and he had never had one. "I'd be a very old lady. Besides, nothing like that is going to happen to your wife, and you shouldn't think about things like that."

"Yes, it will. My mom died. My grandmother died."

"Don't talk like that."

"Your mom died."

"James, go to sleep."

"I guess moms don't live very long."

"Granny D is in her eighties and she's still alive."

He thought about that. "You make a very good point. Don't fall asleep, okay."

I stayed awake until I heard his breathing get shallow. My eyes stayed focused on the window, the darkness outside. The tire swing moved, twisted, as if a child were lazily playing alone. My e y e s *drifted* IN and   out   of *focus* ... **sleep** ...

That night I dreamed of Mama and Granny D in a field on a starlit night. They looked like goddesses. The sky moved like time was speeding up. The stars cycled, but the sky always stayed evening. Granny and Mama each held the hand of a little girl as they walked toward me. The little girl wanted to run but they told her to slow down. There was another woman in the distance. I couldn't make out her face, but she was holding James. When they saw me, she handed James to me. I held out my hand. It was a sturdy branch. James grabbed it. I felt his warm, small hand ...

I woke up. James was holding my arm. Reflected in the windowpane, was my own face, my body cuddled around this little boy. Outside, I saw it near the tire swing. A single yellow flower. My god...

Chapter 17

In Granny D's bedroom is a watercolor drawing of two lovers kissing by the artist Efram T. Corbet, painted when the artist was only fifteen. I was just a child then, but I knew looking at him, the confident way he stood on Granny's porch, his mannerism, that he would be famous. He must be close to fifty years old now, and he is indeed quite famous. I had met his wife Joy once in an airport. She's about my age and a premiere Egyptologist. She's the one who told me the most popular story about Osiris and Isis. The legend is that the body of Osiris, who was killed by his brother, was dismembered and cut into thirteen pieces. Isis, his wife, collected twelve pieces, but could not find the last piece – his penis. She fashioned a golden phallus and used a spell to bring him back to life long enough for her to conceive. Osiris became the god of fertility and rebirth, responsible for flooding the Nile every year. He also protected the dead on the journey to the afterlife. Isis became a goddess, protector of children. Their son Horus, the god of the sky.

"That's worth a fortune," I said, as Granny sipped a cup of

coffee in bed, referring to the painting.

"I like Gracie Ann's painting of the three-legged cat better," she said, pinching off a piece of plain toast. It was early morning, the sun not yet awake, but I knew Granny would be up watching *Spinnin' 4 Winnings*. With my hair a mess, before having a shower, I had made her breakfast in bed. James was still sleeping peacefully in my room; the girls still all tucked in too. Granny had told me she was exhausted, and would it be all right if she spent the day in bed. I told her sure. Get some rest.

"Still," I continued, talking about the artwork, "It's a great story. He was just a teenager, not famous at all, when he gave you that. He traded you for a jar of jam."

She smiled. "Efram has good sense. You can eat jam."

"I met his wife once."

"They're sweet kids. They're on the mailing list."

Granny mails out jam to a select group of people. Bill Clinton is another recipient of free jam. His autographed photo is also on the wall. Not sure if all the recipients request the jam, or if Granny just happens to like them.

She smiled. "You thought Efram was cute."

"I did not." I did.

"Efram's mother used to make muscadine jam. She should have sold it."

"His paintings are very passionate, even that one, and he was just a boy at the time," I said.

"You see that now, do ya? When you were a little girl, you said, 'Granny, frame that. He might be famous some day.' So, I did, but all these years I've never heard you comment on it other than for its monetary value. Gracie Ann does, but she's an artist too." She looked at me, serious. "It's Eddie. That's what makes you see it."

"Granny ... " I stood up. "I need to make breakfast for the kids."

She re-situated herself under the covers, handed me her empty plate and cup. "I'm glad you're with him."

"I'm not *with* him."

"You sure as hell were *with* him last night."

"Granny!"

"Oh, grow up, Faith. You had sex. You need someone. To love someone, that's what makes life worth living. Pops was everything. You've never had that."

"I was married." I sat back down, put her plate and cup on the nightstand.

"Eh! Stephan. The little French twerp. What'd that short fucker know about passion?"

I'm not sure why passion fades, but it's like a photo in the sunlight. It starts out bright, everyone looks at the smiling faces. Eventually, people forget about it, letting it collect dust. Before long, the colors are muted, and you want to replace it with a new photo or a knickknack.

"I did love him, I think."

"You never liked him. That was all about being fancy, shallow, and snooty."

"Maybe."

"It feels different with Eddie. Admit it," she said.

"It doesn't matter anyway. I'm going back to Boston on Monday."

"You think distance changes anything?"

I tapped my fingers on the nightstand. Embraced the crazy. "I saw a yellow flower last night."

Her eyes lit up. "You did? Where?"

"Out by the tire swing. I had a dream, and when I woke up it was there, but it wasn't there before." I told Granny D everything, but I left out the part about her being in the dream.

"Your mother was trying to tell you something, Faith. You should listen, but let me tell you something about Eddie. He's a man trapped between two worlds, the living and the dead. He's like a hot air balloon tied to the ground. He wants to fly up and away, but he's tethered to the land. He's stuck to that woman's grave. Be careful. If you push him, cut those ties quickly like snapping a twig in half, he might fly so far away you won't be able to pull him back."

****

I have to admit that I almost have a fetish with the Beach Boys song *Kokomo*. Whenever I hear it, I have to dance. It's my favorite song, and it played on the radio as I made breakfast. I twirled and I spun as I shuffled about the kitchen, the only one still awake. I heeded Granny's warnings, embraced what Mama was trying to tell me, but when I took a deep breath, all I could think about was what a great day it would be. I embraced the smell of the food cooking, my own perfume, the warm summer air from the open back door. I was Ginger Rogers in my own musical fantasy.

Swirling with skillet in hand, I turned to see a ruffled-haired James standing behind me. I flicked the radio off.

"What are you doing?" he asked, sitting down, his little feet not touching the floor.

"Do you want French toast or Belgian waffles?" I asked him, the most chipper I have ever sounded in my entire life. Somewhere in the far reaches of my vocal chords resides "the accent," the Southern one it took years to vanquish. Being back home, I was starting to sound like JoLynn Perkins, the FWC's resident Southern belle. She cooks up fried chicken and lots of things with grease. Olive oil is foreign to her.

"Ah, a tour of Europe. Let's go to France, mademoiselle," James replied, clasping his hands together.

"Aunt Faith lived in France," Night said, standing in the entranceway.

"Was it fun?" James asked.

"Kind of."

"Have you ever had Mademoiselle Danielle's Parisian Ice Cream?" James asked.

"What's Parisian ice cream?" Night wanted to know. "Like gelato?"

"Ice cream," James said, "but it's from French cows."

"That's stupid," Night said. "A cow is a cow. Besides, I bet they don't have cows in Paris. It's like L.A. or New York. Where are you going to put a cow?" Night stirred the French toast mixture in the bowl. "Can I help make breakfast?"

"Me too. Can I help?" James asked, already certain French ice cream was a myth. "What about French toast? Is it really from France?"

"I don't know, James. In France it's called 'pain perdu', which means 'lost bread'. A long time ago, people made it so they wouldn't waste stale bread."

"Is this bread stale?" Night asked, a little disgusted.

"No. Do you know how to fry it?" I had noticed when we made the strawberry shortcake that Night has a knack for cooking. She takes her time, thinks about how it looks too.

She nodded, but I showed her how to get the edges just right. It makes no sense that I can make perfect French toast, but I burn the buttered skillet toast every time. I left her in charge of the French toast, told her to put bittersweet chocolate chips over them when done, then turned to James. "You're in charge of setting the table. Go outside and pick some flowers. There's a yellow one by the tire swing. Make sure you get that one."

"Yes, ma'am." He saluted. Trotted off. His mission at hand.

Since it was a Saturday; the television flipped on before Lucy made her way into the kitchen. I heard her arguing with Starry, who snatched the remote control. Lucy wanted cartoons; Starry wanted pop bands.

The three of us let the lazy ones relax while we finished cooking. When we were done, we had a great spread laid out. Waffles, French toast, scrabbled eggs, bacon, and sausage. The orange juice and milk were both in glass containers, not jugs and cartons. I hate seeing such tacky things on the table. It only takes five seconds to pour the milk and juice into a nice container. I opened one of Granny D's jam jars, stuck a spoon with a pretty handle in the middle of it. I brought out a crystal vase and made sure the yellow flower went in the middle of the arrangement. The three of us looked at our display. Good enough to eat.

Before the other two kids came into the kitchen, Gracie Ann and Jonesy came in the back door. They had no signs of a hangover and were in good moods too.

"Hey, you made breakfast!" Gracie Ann exclaimed. "Right on."

"Hot tamales and get your lemons! Wow, wow, this looks delicious!" Jonesy said, taking a puff from his pipe. "So artfully arranged."

"Shame we're going to tear into it like pigs," Gracie Ann said as the girls came running in.

Lucy jumped into her father's arms. "You're a little gymnast, that's what you are," he said.

"Are we still going to the mountain?" Lucy asked. "Can James come?"

"We'll have to ask his father, but I'm sure it'll be okay."

They were leaving the next morning and wanted to spend their last day at Pinnacle Mountain in Little Rock, hiking and having a picnic.

"You don't think it'll get too hot out today? It's suppose to be in the nineties," I asked them, holding out a chair for someone to sit down. Starry plopped down.

"Too hot," she said, still depressed from the night before.

"We'll be fine," Jonesy said, famished, digging into breakfast. Just like Gracie Ann said, they all dug in like pigs. I looked at Night, and she had my old familiar "I can't believe I'm related to them" look.

"Where's Granny?" Gracie Ann said. "Is she all right?"

"She's still in bed. She's exhausted. I brought her the paper.

She seems all right. She coughed a lot last night though."

"Maybe we shouldn't leave?"

"I'll be here. Go. Have fun with the kids." I wanted to get rid of them, so I could spend the day with Eddie.

She grabbed a slice of bacon and said, "Let's go out on the steps." Once outside, she said, "I mean, maybe we shouldn't leave yet. Go back to Los Angeles. I'm thinking about asking her to move to L.A. with us."

"She'll never do that."

"She's all alone."

"What about Eddie? I thought you wanted him to move into our house."

She grinned and whispered, "So, our opinion of ol' Eddie is quite different now, eh? How was it last night anyway?"

"I don't know what you're talking about." I folded my arms, feigning ignorance.

"That's odd because I don't recall you and Eddie ever getting into the creek with us. Where did you two run off to?"

"It would be inappropriate to discuss such things," I said, coy smile.

"Yeah? It's also unladylike to roll around in the bushes. Gee, I could have sworn I heard wolves baying somewhere in those woods."

"Were we that loud?"

"Ah-ha! So you admit it!"

We both giggled. To have seen us, it would have been like looking at two preteen girls talking about a boy in *Teen Beat*. I held my knees close to me as we sat on the steps. "He's ... he's great, just great."

"This is so cool! I want all the details. Tell me everything, but quietly." She stood up, looked around. "Come on, let's go out in the field so no one can hear." We walked out to the field, stood among the corn stalks.

I picked up a lump of loose dirt, let it rest in my hand, feeling the coolness. "How was he, you know, when you two?" I asked her.

"Me? What do you mean?"

"When you slept with him. How was it? Losing your virginity ... I can't imagine with ... he's huge!"

"I never slept ... he's huge?"

"Massive."

"Ah!"

"Wait, you never slept with Eddie? You told me you did."

"When?"

"Gracie, you came home, don't you remember, from being at his garage and you were all dreamy-eyed, and the way you put it, he 'taught you something' that changed your life."

"Are you talking about when I stopped smoking weed? That night?" She laughed. "He taught me how to meditate. It was, like, so much more transcendental than pot."

"All these years I thought you ... "

"Nope. Not once."

"Who was your first then?"

"Glen."

"Jonesy! No! Really?"

"Who was yours? Stephan, right?"

"Hell, no! Are you serious? Donnie Thompson. A few days before graduation. I thought you knew."

"Gross. That jock. Wait a minute, you and Mama were always saying how you should wait until you get married. Be proper, respectful. I was considered the wild one, but I waited until my wedding night, and you screwed the football nerd! Hypocrite." She shoved me, playfully.

I shrugged. "Everyone thinks you and Eddie slept together, everyone at school."

"Don't care. Most of those stories about Eddie are made up anyway. He was always with Mindy. He was crazy about that girl."

"He still loves her."

"He doesn't. He's obsessed with her death, not in love." She picked up a twig and threw it. "It's been eight years. He's has to let go." She pulled a husk from a piece of corn. "Maybe he has?"

"I'm going home Monday."

"So."

"Who do you think he was with up by Mulberry Pointe? Did you ever ask him?"

"He hasn't mentioned any girls to me, but he doesn't tell me everything. Why does it matter?" She yanked off a corn cob, let it rest in her hand, felt the weight of it. "Huge, you say?"

"Remember that donkey Poppy got to plow the field?"

She hesitated. "Yes ... "

"Eddie's bigger." I giggled.

"Shit! You're making this up."

My hands held up, I said, "I'm not kidding."

"Shit! Shit! Are you serious?"

"Enormous. I didn't know they could get that big."

There wasn't any cheap whiskey around, but we laughed like we were drunk again.

"Is Jonesy a good lover?" Perverse curiosity.

She acted all snuggly, wrapping her arms around herself, dreamily. "Yeah. But you want to know something funny? When he comes, he says 'Holy Tomatoes!'."

I fell backwards into the corn stalks, laughing. "Geez! How do you keep from laughing?"

"Honestly, it doesn't ever seem that funny at the time." She shrugged then laughed. "When he wants to fool around, and he doesn't want the kids to know what we're talking about, he says 'I sure would like to plant a garden, Tomato Puddin'. Yeah, I sure would'," Gracie Ann said, mimicking Jonesy's distinct voice.

"What's his obsession with tomato references? And tamales and lemons?"

"Beats the hell out of me."

"Wee Ste-fan's was tiny."

"French."

We laughed until our sides hurt. It was still early morning but the muggy summer heat was settling in. A drop of sweat rolled down my neck. We quieted down and I said, "I saw a yellow flower." Then I told her my dream.

"Oh, my gosh, Faith ... "

Chapter 18

There is a bizarre thing that happens in Arkansas. There are so many small towns, places without Starbucks and Old Navy, that the communities get together and rent school buses to drive the locals into Little Rock to visit the mall. Today was school bus day. I passed one on the way to Eddie's. There isn't too much to do in Mulberry Field, but I had a good idea of what Eddie and I might be able to do.

When I pulled into his yard, he was outside washing his truck. Late morning and the heat was miserable. Seeing Eddie felt like a gust of cool wind. He had on a white T-shirt, faded very skin-hugging jeans, and no shoes. Mercy.

The trailer that he had grown up in was far back in the field, falling apart. As a child, Gracie Ann would have played in it, imagining it as an abandoned Mayan temple or something. Weeds surrounded it now, but the rest of the yard wasn't so bad. It needed a little care, but it looked like most yards in the neighborhood. Some patches of grassless dirt, a few shrubs, places where weeds grew out of control. Lots of wildflowers, too. Real ones, not the "weeds" Eddie claimed I picked as a girl. In the center like a vase is a large round yurt made of cedar lattice and a heavy canvass. The porch goes all the way around. I could tell when I pulled up next to Eddie's truck that there was a rectangular shape tacked onto the back, an addition of some sort. His motorcycle, which originally belonged to his father before he skipped town, was still there parked next to a tree. I remembered Eddie riding that to school, knocking the kick-stand down, and mumbling a "hello" to me before slowly making his way to class. When James and I got out of the car, I noticed the motorcycle looked a little rusted. It hadn't been out for a spin in a long time.

Eddie gave me the weak smile he always has and put the water hose down. He came over and picked James up.

"Dad, you're all wet." He squirmed his way out of his father's arms.

"James needs a change of clothes," I said to Eddie. "And he hasn't had a bath or brushed his teeth."

"Is it okay if I go?" He asked his father about the trip to Pinnacle Mountain.

"Sure. I said okay on the phone. Take a bath and change." He playfully spanked James' bottom. "Behave too." James ran to the porch as Edward Sr. came out and scooped him up. His great-grandfather kissed him before James could wiggle away. Edward Sr. waved to me, then sat on the porch with a smoke, while James went in to take his bath.

"Need some help?" I asked Eddie.

"Oh, no. I'm just about done." He picked the hose up, rinsed off the truck.

I put the tailgate down, felt for a dry spot, and sat down. "James got a little scared last night. I thought I was going to have to drive him home in the middle of the night."

"Did he? Yeah, well, he's never really spent the night anywhere."

"Poor little guy. I can't imagine what he's been through. Growing up without a mom."

Like the crisp snap of a dried twig, he said, "He does fine without a mother."

"I know. I was ... just ... "

Rudely, he said, "I didn't have a mother. You grew up without a father. What's your point?"

"He was talking about how mothers always die, that's all. I thought that was sad."

He nodded, a little uncomfortable, looked at his watch. "Look, Faith, it's Saturday, so you know, I teach some kids down at the center. I need to get cleaned up and get out of here."

"Are you busy after? I thought maybe we could do something."

"Aren't you going hiking with them?"

"No, I'm staying with Granny D. She's a little tired. I want to look after her, but you could .... "

"She all right?"

"Yeah, yeah, just a little exhausted I think."

"That's understandable."

"You could come over later if you want. I could make you some lunch after your class."

"I have a lot of things to do around the house today."

"Dinner tonight maybe?"

"I have a gig down at the Whiskey Biskey."

"I'd like to hear you play."

"Come on down, yeah, that'd be fine, if you want."

Awkward, I stood up, waved at Edward Sr. "I'm leaving Monday, Eddie."

"Yeah."

"I might not come home for another twenty years." I said it as a joke.

"That wouldn't surprise me."

"You're not going to say anything about last night?" I whispered.

He put the hose down, walked over to the valve, and turned it off. He pulled me away so his grandfather could not hear. "What do you want me to say?"

"I don't know."

"We had sex. That's it," he said quickly like a firecracker going off before the wick gets to the end.

It felt like being hit in the face with a wet sponge. "That's all? I thought it was a little more than that."

"A little more? You want a little more? Look, I know what's going on. Your mother died, you feel guilty, so now you want to play mom."

I slapped him. He didn't flinch.

"Go back to Boston, Faith. That's where you belong." He kicked over a water-soap-filled bucket. "Every girl wants to be James' mom. He has a mom."

"No, he doesn't."

Edward Sr., having seen the slap, came over and handed us both shiny rocks. "You two shouldn't fight."

"Papa, not now," Eddie said and gave the rock back to him.

"Now is good," Edward Sr. said. "Now is short. Twenty years is a long time."

Completely naked and nonchalant, James stepped outside. His hair was very soapy. From a distance, it looked like a little old lady's white puffy hair. "Dad, we're missing some ... "

"James, get back inside! You know better than to stand outside naked!"

"Naked!" he exclaimed and danced around.

"Get IN the HOUSE!"

"We don't have any conditioner. I need conditioner or my hair gets frizzy. I can't let my betrothed see me this way."

"You're betrothed won't see you at all if you don't get your little behind back in the house."

With a pout, James started to go indoors, but he turned back and said, "There'll be trouble in paradise, kiddo. You just wait and see."

"If she likes you for a superficial reason, James, it's not paradise." Then he looked at me.

"Come inside, Faith. I'll get you a Fizz," Edward Sr. said, patting my back.

"I don't like Fizz," I said, wanting to cry.

"Then I'll get you a donut."

I didn't want donuts either, but I went in anyway. I just wanted to get away from Eddie. From the outside, you would think Eddie's house would be circular inside too, but it feels square. There is a small living room, a bar separates it from the kitchen, and there are three doors that lead to two bedrooms and a bathroom. While the outside was in a bit of disarray, inside was immaculate. Nothing out of place, not a spec of dust. There was one table against the wall that was covered in shiny rocks, surrounded by Christmas lights that were turned on. James had the bathroom door open, still rinsing soap out of his hair. I sat on the futon sofa. On the coffee table was a book of romantic poetry by Eric Pilot, along with E.H. Roger's *The Fabric*, a fable about a young girl's mystical journey. I picked up Pilot's book with its faded leather binding, intentionally making it look old. I flipped it over and saw the logo for Currer, Ellis, and Acton – the same publisher as my cookbooks. Edward Sr. gave me a cinnamon Entenmann's donut, and I put the book down. Eddie stomped into the house, joined James in the bathroom, and slammed the door.

Edward Sr. sat down beside me, getting powdered sugar on the couch as he ate his donut. "Eddie will be so mad, me getting sugar everywhere. He likes everything neat and tidy inside."

"That's not such a bad trait."

"No, but when it gets obsessive, it is." He ate the rest of his donut. I barely picked at mine. "He'll go insane trying to get all the sugar off." Edward Sr. rubbed at the sugary dust, smearing it deeper.

"More you rub, the deeper it goes into the grooves. Pain in the ass to remove it. Eventually, it seeps so far into the cracks, no one can see it." He licked the powdered sugar from his fingers. "It's gone."

"Well, yeah."

"Like Mindy."

"Pardon?"

"My grandson believes he's a killer, a murderer."

"What?"

If lucidity could come on a person as quickly as flicking on a light, it came over Edward Sr. at that moment. He was no longer the weird old man handing out shiny rocks. His head, and I believe his heart too, was as clear as a blue sky. "Eddie's guilt sits there in his gut like the sugar on a donut but it's not sweet. It covers him completely, makes him sick. He killed his mom by being born, killed his wife by getting her pregnant."

"That's crazy. It's not his fault."

"Doesn't matter. He sees it that way. When you have guilt that deep, you can't let go. It's worse and more deadly than a clogged artery. To him, he deceived Mindy in the most heinous of ways. She died having *his* child. He can't let himself betray her again. It's his fault she died. Loving another woman would be akin to cheating on her."

James came out of the bathroom, still naked and very cavalier about it. He went to his room and closed the door. I heard the shower running in the bathroom.

"Are you saying there haven't been any women since Mindy?"

"There've been girls, but he hasn't let himself love anyone until now."

I blushed. "I don't think he loves me."

"I think he's fancied you since he put that cotton puff in your hair."

"You know about that?"

He nodded, grinned. If Eddie let himself really smile, he

would smile like his grandfather. "For him, you were way up there in the sky, unreachable, unattainable, like a star. He could look at you, but that's all." He stomped the ground. "He's down here, rooted. Stars always stay above the field. They can't come down anymore than he can go up there."

But we aren't really stars or fields, I thought. We aren't part of some Egyptian myth or Greek legend. We are people. Together feels like a completed puzzle.

"I came down," I said.

Edward Sr. patted my leg. "You miss your mama."

"I missed everything."

He nodded, then dug around in his pocket. "Have another rock."

"Why do you always give people these?"

"They're pretty." He took a deep breath, lucidity faded.

James came out of his room, dressed now, went to the kitchen and took out a can of Fizz. With a towel wrapped around him, Eddie left the bathroom and went to the bedroom. His hair was damp. I was mad, sad, but I still thought mercy when I saw him.

"James, make sure you wear a hat and bring sun screen. If you don't have any, I'm sure Gracie Ann does. It's really hot out today. You don't want to get a sunburn," I said, sounding like a mother. "Your skin is so fair, you need ... " These were things my mother always said to me. She always had to worry about the sun, carry a hat or an umbrella, bring sun block. She never has to worry about it again. The night sky is cool.

"I have a severed finger," James said, ignoring my advice as kids do. "You want to see?" He went back to the bedroom. I expected another dismembered Barbie doll piece.

"Get your cap!" I yelled after him.

"Just make sure, Faith," Edward Sr. said, lucid again, "that you've come down to be planted. Once that soil surrounds you, you start to grow, you become rooted, part of the landscape. Is that what you really want?"

Eddie came out, readjusting his belt as if he could not get the notches to line up properly. He was dressed in slacks, Stray Cats T-shirt under a long-sleeved denim shirt, and scuffed loafers. A ball cap on his head read "Hot Springs, AR." He looked like a college student, not a teacher. James was behind him and presented me with a severed finger floating in a jar of formaldehyde.

"James, where did you get something like that?"

"Antique store. It's a real human finger. I wonder how he lost his finger? Maybe he donated it to science, or maybe he had no choice? Did you know doctors used to experiment on criminals in the Middle Ages?"

"That's ... very disgusting."

"Can we take Faith antiquing in Keo?" James asked. "You know who I met there? The writer Ryan Ingram. He was buying a piano. I got his autograph. Want to see?" He started to walk off, but turned back. "Are you famous too?"

"Yes."

"You don't seem famous."

"How do I seem?"

"Like a person. Dad, does Faith seem famous to you?"

Eddie couldn't respond. His eyes were on the powdered sugar on the sofa. "Papa, were you eating on the couch? I'll never get that up."

Edward Sr. glanced at me.

"Ready to leave, Faith?" James asked, already forgetting about his celebrity autograph.

"I told you to bring a hat."

Eddie took his off, plopped it on James' head.

Before we left, Edward Sr. said to me, "You want to know why I like shiny rocks, Faith? They live in the earth for so long, it takes a long time for them to form, and when they reach the surface, they're beautiful, each one polished and unique."

Chapter 19

I put on one of Mama's hats. She kept them all in boxes just like women might have done in the days when hats were as much a part of an ensemble as a pair of shoes. I moved it around on my head, trying to get a feel for it, as I looked in the full-length mirror that was on the outside of the closet door. The hat smelled like her hair. Everything in my mother's room smelled like her. Baby powder.

This was the first time I had been alone in the house. There was a hollow sound when I had first opened the door. Gracie Ann and Jonesy had their things strewn about, but it was still Mama's bedroom. Her clothes were in the closet, her purse on the dresser, and her framed photo of Dad by the bed. I had looked at the picture for a moment, realized my cheeks were getting as puffy as his had been. None of his things were in the house, at least not clothes, just Mama's mementos of him. Mama had other boyfriends when we were growing up. One Gracie Ann and I both liked, and it seemed serious at the time. He worked at the electric company and came by once a month to read the meters. On warm days, Mama and Granny D liked to sit outside sipping tea, and they always offered him a glass. One day, he asked Mama out on a date. They went out for a few years until he was transferred as a lineman to Biloxi, Mississippi. He said there was an office job open for Mama, and we could all move, be near the ocean. Mama did not want to leave home or her secretary job at the doctor's office, so he left and we stayed.

Another constant was the pack of gum in Mama's purse. She always had gum. Mama was a big gum chewer. Wrigley's peppermint. I had dug around in the purse, and sure enough, found an opened pack. I took out a piece and chewed it.

I put on another hat. Purple is not my color. Mama liked the dark bright tones, reds, purple, orange. I like black, grey, navy. I found a dark blue hat with a black ribbon. It went really well with my hair color. I pouted my lips which is a funny thing everyone does when they model alone in front of a mirror. Unfortunately for me, Granny D was standing in the open doorway.

"Lovely," she said, startling me. She came into the room, sat on a pile of Gracie Ann's clothes. "It does look nice on you."

"Thanks."

She had something folded up in her hand, papers. She patted the bed, wanting me to sit down. I scooted back the clothes and sat beside her. She handed a set of folded papers to me, kept another set in her hand.

"What's this?" I opened the papers.

"You and Gracie Ann need to look at it before you leave."

"Mama's will," I said, reading over it. She handed me the other set. I opened it. "Your will? Granny, I can't ... "

"No, now, Faith, don't start." She stood up. "Just listen to me and hear me out. I want to make sure that you girls are taken care of, this land stays in your hands. Your mama owned this house and two acres, she left it to you girls, you know that. The rest was in my name, and I'm giving it to you two also. I don't want either of you fighting over ... "

"We'd never do that."

"Going to probate, settling, it's a mess."

"You keep this." I handed her will back. "I don't ... "

She sat back down. Didn't take the papers. "If I were a novel, I'd be on my last few pages, Faith."

"Stop it."

"Getting to the last chapter."

"No, you're not. You're just getting up there in age, that's all."

"Faith, a person knows." She stood up again. "Coming to an end, I am. Time to start a new book. Hope Pops is in it." She said the last part with a smile, but I found nothing to grin about.

I threw Mama's hat to the floor, along with the wills. "Don't say stuff like that! What is wrong with you?"

"Everyone dies, Faith."

"You said that to me already when I was upset about Mama. Why can't you fight death tooth and nail like everything else?"

"Nothing can stay the same. You know how many times I've plowed and harvested that field out there? Too many times to count. Wouldn't be much of a garden, now would it, if it was just a one-timer, stayed the same field forever? Be rather dull. It has to be plowed, planted, and plucked every year. Cycle of life, Faith. It's the only way."

"I don't want to hear this."

"You never do."

"Bull. I was just starting to deal with Mama, and letting go, and Eddie, and coming back, and now you say ... no, I'm not listening." Rage came out of me like a crazy person. I stood up, threw Gracie Ann's clothes on the floor, swiped the dresser clean with my arm, and kicked over the stack of hat boxes. "This is why I don't come home! I can't stand it here! I just can't! Madness! Nothing is ever sane or normal. There's always something. Always something to worry about!" I looked at her with hate, stomped the crap out of the hat boxes. "I always had to worry about Mama growing up. Worry she might die because of some stupid disease that didn't make sense. What'd you and Poppy do? Huh? Worry about your stupid Weston feud! *It's just jelly.*"

"I know it's just jelly, Faith."

"No, no, you don't. You worry about silly things. Who gives a shit that she has her jelly in Safeway? You think I didn't care about Mama, because I haven't been home in twenty years, because you were with her when she died? Let me tell you something, Granny, I was here every damned fucking day after school, hoping, praying, that if I was a good girl, made sure I did my homework, washed the dishes for her, kept the house tidy, that she'd come home from work at all ... that I wouldn't get a phone call that said she had died, her kidneys gave out, or her lungs stopped working, her body gave up on her. I didn't give up on her." I pulled the curtains off the window. You know how even as an adult, if you get really scared, you still want your mother? I no longer had one to get. I ran out of the room, down the hall, through the living room, and outside. I kept running, far into the woods, until I reached the old tree house. There were only a few boards there, still tacked to that tree. I sat under it. A long time. It just got hotter and I couldn't take that anymore either.

When I walked into Granny D's kitchen, she had a pitcher of lemonade waiting. She poured me a glass as I sat down.

"Get it all out?" she asked, sitting beside me.

I shook my head. "I shouldn't have yelled at you. I didn't mean it."

"Ya did. It's okay. I thought you and Gracie Ann were spoiled little brats leaving me here to care for her. We all have resentments. Big deal, doesn't mean we don't still love each other."

"I thought I had dealt with everything. That I could move on."

"You can't move on from death. It's always goin' to hurt. It just doesn't hurt as much over time. I still cry about Pops. You think I don't?" She got real close to me and whispered, "I want to see him again real bad."

"I don't want you to go."

"I don't want to leave, but, eh, what can ya do about it?"

"Are you sick, Granny, or are you talking nonsense? Just tell me the truth."

"I'm old."

"Some people live to be a hundred."

"I don't want to live that long. I'd end up looking like Ruthie Weston."

"I'm sorry about what I said."

She patted my hand. "It is just jelly." She took a drink. "Tell me what happened with Eddie. You seemed a little down when you came back."

"I pushed him too hard like you told me not to."

She sighed. "That boy. He's the complete opposite of you. You keep wanting to release death, and he can't give it up."

"He thinks he's responsible for their death, his mom and Mindy."

"I know. He's crazy as a betsy bug."

Realization hit me. She had a piece of the puzzle. "Who's Janet?"

She scratched her head. "A girl. Down at the Whiskey Biskey. Waitress there."

"He dates her?"

"Eh, he sleeps with her."

"He has a show tonight."

She slapped her leg. "Go down there and get your man. Puff up those boobs, get gussied up, put on something slinky." Granny D slid her hand down her body, making a sexy gesture.

"I can't do that!"

"Gracie Ann and Jonesy will go with you. I'll stay with the girls."

"I don't think he wants me ... "

CRASH. Something smashed through the kitchen window.

Granny picked it up. A brick with a piece of paper around it. I saw the silver Cadillac driving away. Ruthie Weston. Granny read the note: *Jelly thief. Did you find out what jelly should taste like?* Gracie Ann and Jonesy had taken the box of strawberry jelly with them to Little Rock. They planned to find a deserted place along the Arkansas River to dispose of it.

Calmly, Granny threw the paper away, put the brick outside. "You want me to take the high road? End this thing? It is just jelly."

"No, I want to kick her ass." I thought about it. "And I want to kick Janet's ass too. What does she look like anyway?"

"Skanky."

"I want that man, Granny, but I don't want to push him too hard. I want him like I've never wanted any man ever. I want to be with him, have kids with him, live with him, share life with him. Everything."

"Passion. See," she said, "that's how it should feel."

"But, Granny, I'm leaving on Monday."

Chapter 20

In high school Darren Hasselcock Clay was a tattletale. He
was always the outsider, never one of the cool kids, never a member of
any clique. He wasn't a geek, a jock, a joker, an artist, a smart one. He
was just annoying. Now he mans the door at the Whiskey Biskey. Just
like in school, he enjoys pushing people around, being the gatekeeper.
Above his head, as he watched each person enter, was a large sign that
said "Eddie Field and the Live Jive."

I approached Darren with Gracie Ann and Jonesy. He had
never tattled on me as I was always the most perfect, the most moral,
the most popular in school. Sure he tried, but it was a dry well. Gracie
Ann, he got dirt on her all the time. I would assume he ratted on Eddie,
too. Now he stands outside, while Eddie stands on stage. Life.

"Looky there, if it isn't the town's very own celebrity come
home," Darren said.

"Hi, Darren," I said, as phony as I could. "You haven't

changed a bit." He has a gold tooth and too much cologne.

"Here to see Eddie? Hello, Gracie, how are you? Is this the ball and chain?"

Jonesy shook hands like a mover-and-a-shaker. "Nice to meet you, yeah, I guess I am the old ball and chain. Yup. This is the little woman, my Tomato Puddin'. Wow, nice place you got here. Yeah, real nice. I could shoot a picture show here."

"You make films?"

"Big films. Big stars. Yeah. Who do I talk to about shooting a picture here?"

"That'd be Big Bob Hunter. He runs the joint."

Jonesy pushed his way inside, on the hunt for Hunter. If this was the same "Big Bob" Hunter who was two years older than me, he would not be easy to convince about making a picture. He has the temperament of a pit bull, the personality of a Tasmanian devil, and the looks of a lumberjack. In school, we called him "The Man," because he had a full beard by age twelve.

When we walked in, Eddie and his band, which was no small affair, were in the middle of a rockabilly swing version of Stevie Ray Vaughan's *The House is Rockin'*. With a voice like Jonny Lang, charismatic Eddie played a guitar that looked like B.B. King's Lucille. Accompanying him on upright bass was Peter Boyd, who looks like Brian Setzer and was good friends with Eddie in school. On bass guitar was Jack Webb, wearing a railroad cap, and his wife Christie, former high school sweethearts, in a pink bucket hat on the drums. The twins Jim and Tim Brooks were on sax. Amy Brinkley played trumpet, but I didn't recognize the other trumpet player, who looked like a new wave singer with big curly hair parted to one side. The band was rounded out by a keyboard player named Wiedlin, who looks like Chaka Khan, and two trombone players dressed in 1940s business suits. The band geeks made cool.

I got close to the stage, but Eddie didn't see me. He was dressed his usual way with jeans and a faded T-shirt, but the lights, music, and guitar made him look like a rock star. Back to back with Jack, they went to town on the song. I felt the same way I had when I first saw Efram T. Corbet standing on Granny's porch when he was young. He's going to be a star.

"He's incredible!" Gracie Ann said, clapping her hands, wiggling to the beat. "Didn't I tell you?"

He was definitely something. I hoped he appreciated the skin-hugging number I picked up at the dress shop in the strip mall earlier in the day. It made me feel sexy and invincible. Gracie Ann saddled her way over to the bar, ordered some drinks, while Jonesy harassed Big Bob, who seemed to cozy up to the idea of his place being in a "picture show." I saw waitress Janet pretty early on. She wasn't hard to spot. Big hair, big boobs, big ass. Her name tag said "Janet" and she recognized me too.

"Oh, my gosh! Faith Orion! So exciting! I love your show."

Charming, I thought, now go away. "Thank you. That's very sweet."

"Eddie's told me so much about you, how you two went to school together. So exciting!"

"Really?"

"Is that Gracie Ann?" she asked as Gracie came over and handed me a drink. "Eddie talks about you too. Your husband is a director! That's so exciting!" She grabbed Gracie Ann's hand and shook it real hard. Jonesy walked over, pleased with his badgering, and shook Janet's hand too. She said, "A director! So exciting! You must know so many stars."

In some ways Janet was nice, maybe a little phony, but not what I expected. Still, I rightfully hated her.

"Isn't Eddie great? He's such a rock star!" she said, ogling him.

"Yeah, he's great." Now die, bitch.

"You could put Eddie in a movie," Janet said to Jonesy.

"Eddie would be great. Yeah. A real star, he is," Jonesy said, moving only his shoulders when he danced.

My upper hand was that Janet didn't know she was suppose to be fighting for Eddie. It's like being cold-cocked over the head from behind. She never knew it was coming. Oblivious, she told us to enjoy the show, winked at Eddie, and sashayed off.

"Skank," Gracie Ann whispered to me. "That dress is K-Mart all the way. You're so much prettier than her. Did you see her make-up? Goodness. What's Eddie thinking?"

Eddie was thinking about me being there, because I caught his glance. I didn't have to be a music major to get that he missed a beat. He grimaced, but caught up, and did not look my way again.

When Gracie Ann and family had come home from Pinnacle Mountain, I told her about everything that had happened with Eddie and the stuff Granny told me about the wills. The entire day had been filled with ups and downs. I wanted to relax and enjoy the concert, but the look Eddie gave me made my head pound.

"Gracie, do you think this is stupid?"

"What? No," she yelled back over the music, dancing and drinking. She knows how to rock out.

"Let's just go. He doesn't want me here."

The red dress had no power. No effect on Eddie. I was not invincible. Or sexy. Big Bob Hunter liked the outfit though. He kept giving me the eye.

"Faith, stay. You have to talk to him."

"Are we leavin', Tomato Puddin'?" Jonesy asked, not able to hear the entire conversation over the music.

"Faith wants to leave."

"Why? He's great. Real great." He snapped his fingers. "Hey, we could toilet paper Ruthie Weston again after this."

"No more TP. I just want to go home. I need to pack."

"You've got another day to pack," Gracie Ann said, guzzling the liquor like a glass of water.

"I've decided to go home tomorrow. There's no need to stay."

I grabbed her arm, pulled her away from the front of the stage. Jonesy followed. As if on cue, the music stopped. The three of us turned back, listening to the thunderous applause.

"Wado. Thank you. We're takin' five. Be back in a minute or so," Eddie said, saluted and walked off the stage.

"Stay, Faith," Gracie Ann said, yanking me back. "Just talk to him. Go! Now."

I didn't have to. Eddie came over to us.

"Hey," he said to all three of us. "Leaving so soon?"

"We have to pack. We're leaving in the morning," I said.

"I thought you were leaving Monday?"

"I decided to fly out tomorrow. No need to stay any longer. Everything's done." I said it as unemotional and cool as I could. I was an iceberg, cold and unmovable.

He nodded, patted his legs, nervously. Janet came over, threw her arms around him, and gave him what seemed like a million kisses on the cheek, getting her lipstick cooties all over his face. "You were so great!" she said. "Wasn't he great? It's so exciting!" Is there nothing that doesn't excite this girl? Paint drying? A pin dropping maybe. But I'm not sure. Eddie shrugged and pulled away from her. "Okay, then," he said to us. "If I don't see you before tomorrow, goodbye then. Thanks for coming down."

He leaned over to hug Gracie Ann, but before he could, she exclaimed, "Faith's in love with you!"

There was that pin drop. Remarkably, Janet did not find this the least bit exciting. "What?" she said.

I turned as red as the dress. "I need to go."

Gracie Ann expunged everything like a continuous roll of computer paper printing at breakneck speed. "Eddie, I've known you forever and I know you feel the same way and this bullshit has to end because I think you two belong together and you have to let Mindy go and, Faith, tell him the dream!"

"What's this shit?" Janet said still confused, eyeing me now.

Not such a fan anymore.

"We had sex. Nothing more," I said it looking at Janet, but I meant it for Eddie's ears. I intended it to be hateful to both.

I walked out. Eddie let me go. He did not belong in my world, and he wouldn't let me into his.

That night I sat under the stars at my old house, on our old porch, and realized it was like being on that train platform the day I left for college. I would not be coming back. I asked Gracie Ann to give me some of Mama's hats; I wanted to take them with me. I packed a few photos too. Gracie Ann planned to come back later in the summer to sort out Mama's things, see what to sell, what to keep. She didn't ask about Eddie staying at the house again, but she did ask Granny to move to L.A. The answer was no.

Chapter 21

The Little Rock airport is very small, but Gracie Ann and family ended up on the far end, so we hugged goodbye before they trotted down to their gate. A part of me thought that Gracie Ann might smirk and flip me the bird like she had all those years ago at the train depot. She didn't though. She just hugged me the same way she might have done if I were flying back to Boston after visiting L.A. She did have a "knowing" look on her face just like Mama had that day, but it was me that was oblivious to what it meant. Jonesy patted me briskly, always lost in movieland. I gave Night some recipes, and she promised to try them out. Starry watched another teenage boy walk by and waved to me, following him without his knowledge. Lucy jumped into my arms, and I kissed her cheek. She already missed her betrothed.

When we had left Granny's house, we made sure she would be okay alone. Still a little tired, she told us, but she promised to call Eddie or Ol' man Wilson if she felt bad. She loaded us both up with mulberry jam. My suitcase felt like a brick. I packed it with lots of newspaper, hoping the jars would not break.

I sat alone in the terminal. Called my secretary Brad. Things had "gone to pot" without me there, he said. The show started taping soon, and some of the ideas for next season were "off the wall" he told me. My thoughts, though, were not with cooking, or ratings, or television. I kept smelling mulberries. I got up and went to the bakery in the food area.

"Are those mulberry muffins?" I asked the clerk.

"Mulberry? No, blueberry. Hey, you're Faith Orion!" He grabbed a napkin. "Sign this."

I signed it. "Do you smell mulberries?" I asked him.

"Honey, I don't know what a mulberry smells like."

I did. And it was there.

He leaned over, sniffed me before I left. "I think it's you."

I looked at my watch. It had stopped. The time said 3:03 p.m., but I knew it was close to three thirty. My plane would be leaving soon. I passed the bookstore. A copy of my cookbook was in the window, along with a star field guidebook with a picture of Orion. I smiled at that. The bookstore probably didn't even realize it. Gracie Ann would have loved it. I was turning into her. I was seeing signs. A child walked past, eating a biscuit from the bakery. She dropped it, and it rolled past me. I went to Gracie Ann's terminal; her flight had already boarded.

"Eddie," I said into my cell phone, "can you pick me up at the airport? There aren't anymore trains today, and I don't want to take a cab."

An hour and a half later, I was in his truck. We didn't say much, but he asked if I was hungry, and we stopped at Sonic for burgers, fries, and cherry Cokes. As we ate, he said, feeling a little awkward, "I'm sorry about what I said to you. I shouldn't have ... been so cold. It's really hard for me, to even go there, but I didn't have the right to be so hateful to you. I'm sorry, Faith. I hope you can forgive me."

I shuffled in my seat. "It's okay. I understand. You're probably right. I just got caught up in everything." I took a sip of Coke. I wasn't going to push him. It's like being on a tire swing as a child. You have to learn to get in the air on your own before you want someone to push you up high.

"It's been a long time, you know, for me," I said. "Stephan, well, he was ... blah."

He nodded a little, laughed a little. "Yeah."

"Friends?"

"Sure." We shook on it. He ate a few more fries and joked, "If you're going to pal around with me, you have to stop being so stuck-up. I won't tolerate it."

"What? I'm not snobby! Why does everyone say that?"

He threw up his hands. "You are. Look at the way you're sitting."

"What's wrong with the way I'm sitting?" Not really offended.

"Perfectly! Hands clasped, knees together, tiny little itty bitty bites. You eat ... slowly."

I crossed my arms. "Fine." I took a big bite of the burger and a glob of ketchup fell onto my shirt. "See, look, a mess."

"I didn't say anything about getting messy."

"Oh, you don't like that?" With my finger, I took the glob of ketchup and smeared it on his shirt.

"I'll never get that out."

"You're as picky as me. Admit it and I'll tell you how to get ketchup stains out."

"No." Resolute.

Mocking his voice, I added, "Oh, Papa, I'll never get the couch clean."

"You don't know what it's like living with him! He's a pig!"

"Trust me, I do!"

We both laughed. He finished his drink, pondered for a moment, tapped the steering wheel. "What was the dream? The one Gracie Ann said you had," he asked, only giving me one quick glance, trying to be nonchalant.

I smiled. "Another day, Eddie. Another day, okay?"

He nodded, looked me in the eye. The rearview mirror fell down.

****

When we pulled into the yard, Granny D was on the front porch. She saw the truck, shook her head, and stood up. "I was a lookin' forward to some rest and relaxation," she said.

I got out of the truck. "You got me instead."

"If you're a goin' to stay awhile," she said as Eddie carried my luggage into the house, "I'm puttin' you to work."

"I thought I could get a head start on getting Mama's things together."

I never did get around to doing that though. I spent the next couple of weeks talking to Granny D. We sat on the front porch, sipping tea, talking about nothing really. When the man came to read the electric meter, we offered him tea too. I showed Granny how to make a hollandaise sauce; she showed me how to get the buttered skillet toast just right. I learned that when she was a little girl, she broke her foot falling down some stairs. I had never heard that story before. She wore a cast for a long time, and when they took it off, she felt like she had to learn to walk all over again. She told me Mama once stuck a piece of saltwater taffy in Uncle John's hair; Mama proceeded to give him a "hair cut" to hide the evidence, only to make it far worse. Before they were married, Poppy liked to kiss Granny underneath this canopy at a ballpark, and he had a complex about his big toe, he thought one was too big. Dad had a complex about his ears being too small. The first time Dad officially proposed to Mama, on bended knee during a candlelight dinner, she turned him down, only to call him up later to say yes. All these things, I would never have known if I had flown back to Boston, gone back to being Chef Faith Orion, star of the FWC, with no Southern accent, a misplaced puzzle piece.

The Fields came over often. Granny and I made dinner, but Eddie always brought the drop biscuits and an alcoholic cider he made with Ol' man Wilson's apples. James liked to play on the tire swing; he still missed his betrothed and kept in touch via email. Edward Sr. and Granny D gossiped, thought of ways to annoy Ruthie Weston. Eddie and I never brought up our romp in the thicket at Old Rice Creek. We kept our relationship lighthearted and friendly, but one hot day, as I picked tomatoes in the field, the taping of my next season looming on the horizon, Eddie came up behind me. I saw he had a gold chain hanging from his neck.

"You goin' back soon?" he asked, sitting beside me, pulling tomatoes from the vine.

I nodded. "The network did a focus group, and I'm cooking more 'home style' fair this season."

He smiled. "Granny's food?"

"I've been working on a few things. They said I came off as snobby and unapproachable. The average person doesn't relate to me."

He laughed, a real hearty laugh. "No. Not you!"

"I know, can you believe it?"

I thought he was picking the tomatoes without really paying attention. "You're picking the green ones," I said.

"I like green ones. I like fried green tomatoes."

"I can make them." I brain stormed for a minute. "I could snaz up the recipe, use some spices, maybe put guacamole ... "

"Snobby and unapproachable to the average person." He nudged me with a smile.

"Or I could just fry them in corn meal."

He nodded, held up a tomato. "Green is my favorite color."

"It goes with your eyes." I felt embarrassed for having said it but he smiled. "My favorite color is black."

"I've never heard anyone say that before," he said and touched my hair. "Goes with your hair."

"I can make them for you, fried green tomatoes, if you want."

"Wado," he said. Eddie reached under his shirt, pulled out the gold chain. Hanging from it was his wedding ring. "Is this okay?" he asked. I nodded.

"I'll be home for Thanksgiving," I told him. With those big green eyes, he looked into mine, and he smiled, a full smile. Baby steps.

Chapter 22

I stepped off the train onto the platform in Mulberry Field. I just taped my last show in Boston. My family was waiting for me, my husband Eddie, stepson James, and our two-year-old daughter Karlene Orion-Field. I mixed my grandmother's name Marlene with my mother's name Karen, but we call her Karly for short. She has fair skin, green eyes, and unruly black hair. I think she's going to be like her aunt Gracie Ann; she enjoys playing in the dirt, searching the kitchen cabinets as if they were a jungle, and gnawing on anything she can find. She has absolutely none of our tidy habits and becomes very annoyed when I try to clean her up. Maybe she'll grow out of it? Either way, I don't care. I love her just the same. And, yes, she is that same little girl I saw in my dream. Before she was born, I told Eddie about that, but he still made me wear an "amulet" of the Egyptian god Bes that Gracie Ann had given to me just to be safe. I'm not sure if it was the mythical god's help, but giving birth to Karly was the most fearless thing I have ever done. I had no stress, no doubts, no worries about this little person who harvested in me a love I never thought I would feel.

Once my little shadow, Lucy is starting to take after her mother instead, which probably happens to all of us eventually. She's taken up painting, but Gracie Ann said she's really "taken up making messes." James and Lucy broke off their engagement now that they're cousins. They still email every day, and it's probably good they live so far away. When they get together they are hellions. Lucy is long over her crush on Patrick Swayze, but she still wants to be a dancer and wears pink tap shoes. Sammy Davis Jr. is her new favorite person. The twins are about to get their driver's permits; Los Angeles freeways will be even scarier. "Just like Aunt Faith," Night is turning into quite the chef. She enrolled in a special culinary school for teens and tests her creations on her family. I'm hoping she will make a few things for all of us at Thanksgiving. Starry, long over the Weston boy, is "in love" with her English teacher, a certain Dr. Burt Atwell Taylor, who is "oh-so-dreamy" and looks like a 1920s writer. Their parents are doing well, too. Gracie Ann displayed her "designer sheets" as "art" in a gallery on La Cienega Boulevard in West Hollywood. She's the talk of the town with a variety of celebrities wanting her to make their bed sheets. Hollywood. Go figure. Still extroverted, still friendly, Jonesy has yet to make a "picture show" at the Whiskey Biskey, but he did use the folk dancing barn. He still owes the Wiccan owner ten grand for damages. He'll probably be able to make good on his debt though; he recently coerced an unsuspecting A-list actor to appear in one of his films. As part of the deal, he gets his designer bed sheets for free. Uncle Henry signed on for a small role as, you guessed it, a Madonna impersonator. I'm going to let Jonesy come on my show, too. I've discovered that he makes a fine kabob. People relate to kabobs. Everyone likes a good homemade kabob straight from the grill. The grandparents Orion are thinking about moving back to Arkansas. Grandpa Orion is seeing an acupuncture doctor who claims to be able to help with the arthritis and

Grandpa's magnetism. I think the doc is a quack. The people at the patent office still think Grandma Orion is nuts and have no plans to send her any royalties. She fights on. Aunt Jane and Uncle John promise to visit at Christmas. Not sure about cousin Tootie, although Gracie Ann and I think she'll be recovering from her breast implants. We hear they are double-D. Maude would be so jealous; she's still sacking groceries and trying to keep those tits out of sacks. The last time I saw her, she commented on my lipstick, Sexy Midnight. I brought her a tube from Boston. I think she's sweet on Edward Sr.; her car has been parked outside the yurt on more than one occasion. Ol' man Wilson passed away last year, along with Bob from the train station. Bob's grandson Joseph manages the station now and runs the cab, a spanking new Honda Accord with fancy rims on the tires.

Joseph nodded to us. We were the only people there, and he knew we didn't need a ride. I scooped Karly into my arms and ruffled James' hair (he's gotten so tall). Eddie put his arm around me – underneath his tattoo for James, he has one for Karly too. He kissed me and said, "Osiyo," which is a friendly greeting in Cherokee like "aloha" in Hawaiian. He keeps teaching me new words. With Post-it notes, he sticks them on Granny D's kitchen utensils, the flour, the Kenmore fridge. When I start taping my new show at Granny D's house, I'm not taking them down. I also plan to wear one of Mama's fancy hats every episode. The "home style" fair was a big hit, and the FWC was overjoyed with the concept for my new program – *Faith Orion's Southern Cookin'*. The title is a lie. It's Granny D's food. I don't think she would mind though. She passed away before Karly was born. We flew her pajama bottoms up on the flagpole at Mulberry Pointe. The entire town came out for her funeral. The artist Efram T. Corbet and his wife Joy sent a bouquet of homegrown flowers that sprout, miraculously they say, around their Georgia home. Granny D's house is now a studio, preserved in time, every knickknack to remain the same. Ice cream sandwiches still in the storage room freezer. Jam jars and pectin neatly arranged. Gracie Ann's childhood painting still on the wall. Jake the dog lounging on the sofa without permission.

The red brick house down the long driveway/road has changed quite a lot. James has Gracie Ann's old room, and it's riddled with bizarre and ghastly artifacts that I'm not sure how he procures (too scared to ask). Karly has my old room. It's still dainty and pink, but I feel that won't last. She'll grow up to do her own thing, be her own person, and that's the way it should be, too.

We combined our fields. The Dunley property and the Field land are one and the same. Eddie Sr. stays in the yurt though. We re-modeled it for him; he likes living in something round. He has more room for his rock collection now that Eddie and James have moved out. The place glistens like a piece of flint, especially with the Christmas lights he leaves up all year. Wildflowers bloom all over the place. Yel-low ones pop up at the oddest of times. Maybe they are a sign? Pretty either way. Sometimes I catch a cotton puff drifting by on the ground, and I pop it in my hair. Eddie likes that. Sometimes I get him to laugh, really cackle, and that makes me smile. He still plays down at the Whiskey Biskey, but I like it best when he plays for just me and the kids under the night sky, shadows from a bonfire flickering on his face. Eddie doesn't have the need to visit the cemetery as much as he used too, but we put flowers on the graves on holidays. Mindy's wedding ring is in a box in James' dresser drawer. Eddie wears a silver one now, circled in black stones. Mine is silver too, but surrounded in emeralds.

Eddie got a new truck; the gear doesn't stick and it shifts into forward just fine. He stays busy; the auto shop has really grown, and he wants to keep Granny D's garden – the corn, purple hull peas, and tomatoes – but I told him it's his responsibility. He wants a crop of wa-termelons, too. It will be good to use homegrown produce on the show. The first thing I plan to make is mulberry jam. James loves picking the berries, and Karly likes smashing them on her fingers, turning her little digits purple. My manager thinks I need to market the jam, sell it in stores everywhere with an entire line of Orion products – frozen foods, kitchen utensils, and more. Ruthie Weston would just die.

On the drive home, we passed Mulberry Pointe. Granny's favorite pajama-flyin' flagpole isn't there anymore, but don't worry, the Dunleys, Orions, and Fields still embrace the crazy, each other, our past, and our future. As we reached our home, I could see Orion's belt. All three houses on our property line up perfectly like those pyramids on the Giza Plateau. It's not gods or goddesses that look down on us though. My loved ones live in the constellations, and I look up at them every night. Maybe that's crazy, but maybe not.

Michelle Cushing is the author of *From a Vine*, the well-received novel published in 2007. She graduated magna cum laude with a Bachelor of Arts in journalism and has published many articles. Currently, she is working on her third novel and collaborating on screenplays with her sister XT, the author of *The Mask of Aubrey Clover*.

www.ingramcontent.com/pod-product-compliance
Lightning Source LLC
Chambersburg PA
CBHW020334110726
47898CB00003B/868